# Flames of the Sun

Scott Reeves

Published by Scott Reeves, 2016.

# Flames of the Sun

# Books by Scott Reeves

The Big City

Demonspawn

Billy Barnaby's Twisted Christmas

The Dream of an Ancient God

The Last Legend

Inferno: Go to Hell

Zombie Galaxy: The Outbreak on Caldor

Scruffy Unleashed: A Novella

Colony

A Hijacked Life

The Dawkins Delusion

The Newer New Revelations

Death to Einstein!

Apocalyptus Interruptus: A Novella

The House at the Center of the Worlds

The Miracle Brigade

Tales of Science Fiction

Tales of Fantasy

The Chronicles of Varuk: Book One

Soldiers of Infinity: a Novelette

Welcome to Snowybrook Inn

Snowybrook Inn: Book Four

Liberal vs. Conservative: A Novella
Temporogravitism and Other Speculations of a Crackpot
A Crackpot's Notebook, Volume 1

# 01 - The Feeding

Long ago, in a past so distant and fading that its light has nearly red-shifted beyond all hope of remembrance, the stars fell to the surface of First Home and became flesh, and thus the first men emerged into sapience. In those long-gone days when men were new, most of them flamed daily. But a handful flamed not with the incandescence of light, but of life, and these were the Ashenfolk.

— *The Book of Light*, by Ba'rath'ma'oor.

Embra stared up the tunnel at the gates, two rusted iron doors that barred the tunnel and kept her and the other Flamers penned within their warren.

Today, she was determined to witness a feeding. She could feel the hungry Darkers as dots of emptiness, like black holes pulling at her across the distance, approaching the gates from the other side.

She lurked behind a table that had been tipped over onto its side about twenty feet from the gates. This part of the Pen, being so near to the entrance of the Darkers, was not well-kept, and was littered with detritus such as the battered table that shielded her. Other junk was scattered nearby: two broken chairs; coiled bedsprings that perhaps were the remnants of a long-decayed mattress; the torn and soggy pages of a book, perhaps a bit of literature forbidden by the Darkers which they had discovered in someone's possession and torn apart.

The metal walls of the tunnel were rusted and alive with green mold, with rivulets of oily, noxious liquids that leaked from between gaps in the plates. Liquids from cracked or burst pipes hidden in the infrastructure above, or that had trickled down from the surface through nooks and crannies. The liquid collected in stagnant puddles that dotted the tunnel floor. She could hear a rhythmic drip-drip-drip and a muffled trickling behind the walls as the slow flow continued unabated just as it had for the entire fifteen years of her life. Or at least as much of it as she could remember.

Her nostrils flared with nervousness at the creeping approach of the still-unseen Darkers, and she grew slightly dizzy from the familiar, ever-present stench of oil and mold and rusted iron.

The gas lamps, which hung at intervals along the walls casting their wan yellow light, flickered and went out one by one, as the gas feeding them was cut off at the source, plunging the tunnel into pitch darkness. Darkers did not like light. They could tolerate it if they had to, but she had heard that to them, it was like the most disgusting, offensive stench imaginable. All light except one particular type, that was.

She could hear them now, on the other side of the gates. A metallic click as a lock disengaged; a grinding of metal as a gear turned, and a *thunk* as a bolt retracted. A loud crack as a seal was broken, followed by a further grinding of metal as the gates swung slowly open.

In the darkness, she could not see them. But she could still sense them as points of emptiness, moving up the tunnel toward her. Her mother, now years dead, had once told her that her ability to sense when Darkers were near was unusual, and should not be spoken of openly. Just as the other thing she sensed constantly shouldn't: something far above her. Not an emptiness like the Darkers, but rather an *imminence*, a potentiality, a sense of something waiting. Something that made small movements as though confined to a narrow location. *Was* it a thing, or was it a person? And another something, of the same sort, but larger, more powerful, further distant and moving at great speed, circling her as if tracing out a boundary to the world. Something that made a complete circle in an amount of time that corresponded exactly with the unchanging time period which those in the Pens called "a day."

"Why do none of the others sense these things?" Embra had once asked her mother.

"Because you're special, darling," her mother had said as Embra scrubbed her back.

They were alone in the communal bath, a cavernous room with a huge pool of clean water which took up most of the space. Well, not entirely clean water: there was the ever-present mixture of liquids trickling down the moldy metal walls. Her people tried to keep the noxious streams from contaminating the pool, but a small amount inevitably made it through their makeshift dams.

"But don't ever tell anyone why you're special," her mother had continued. "Such words would surely make their way to the ears of the Darkers, God damn their leathery hides, and our future would die."

Mother reversed positions with Embra, and began scrubbing her daughter's back. A cold, wet finger tapped the birthmark between Embra's shoulder blades: long tongues of flame emanating from a star.

"And most especially don't ever let anyone see this," her mother had cautioned her. "One day everyone will see it, and know just how special you are. But for now, this mark means death for you."

"But Mother," Embra had said. "Why would I tell anyone I'm special when I don't even know *why* those things make me special?"

"Exactly, precious," her mother had said with a sad smile.

"Tell me," Embra had insisted. "Why can I do these things? What is the meaning of my birthmark?"

"When it's time," Mother had replied.

But Mother had died shortly after, leaving Embra with nothing but unanswered questions and a fear of discovery that bordered on paranoia.

Now, Embra could not only sense the Darkers, she could hear them as they passed her hiding place in the darkness. The rustle of their membranous wings, the rhythmic clack of their clawed feet upon the metal floor.

She wondered if they could see her crouching behind the table as they passed. Did they have some other way of seeing than sight? Could they somehow sense her nearness as she could sense theirs? Maybe. Her people knew so little about them, and she knew even less, as she'd stayed on the fringes of the community since her mother's death. Partly by her own choice, since keeping to oneself made it less likely that others would discover that she was special, whatever sort of special she might be. And partly because since her mother's death, as she had grown, it had become increasingly more difficult to conceal her growing abilities, and so they were slowly pushing her away, setting her apart. Everyone was gradually becoming aware that she was special, even if they didn't openly acknowledge it.

It had become an unspoken secret. She couldn't be certain the others knew, and they couldn't be certain that she knew that they knew. That was the nature of secrets. So they all kept quiet about it.

The Darkers passed, a long stream of them. This particular Pen served a community of five hundred, and the morning feeding was usually the most crowded.

After two hundred had streamed past, the line thinned out. One of the stragglers stopped beside the table and sniffed. She heard its thin tongue licking its lipless slit of a mouth.

Embra tensed, preparing to flee.

She had never been this close to a Darker before. His emptiness, the only thing about him visible to her in the pitch blackness, sucked at her, tried to pull something from deep within her. He was a hole in the universe, a hunger, and she fought its instinctive attempt to consume her.

"Can't you smell? She's too young," one of its friends said. Its voice, like all Darker voices, was harsh and grating, almost like the sound of the gates grinding open. "Hasn't yet flamed. Now move on, or let me ahead of you. I'm hungry."

So they couldn't sense her like she could them. She filed that away for future reference. But they could smell her.

The one who had stopped moved away, heading toward the nearby Feeding Room.

Embra relaxed. She had figured they would leave her alone. Why bother with an immature Flamer that couldn't yet nourish you? Most Darkers weren't purposefully cruel; they didn't play with their food.

But it had been a gamble, albeit a safe one. And she had won.

She waited a few minutes to make sure all the Darkers had had enough time to pass through into the Feeding Room. Then, feeling her way through the darkness, she moved up the tunnel and around the corner. Light spilled into the tunnel from an open hatch up ahead, so she no longer stumbled blindly in darkness.

She sidled up to the hatch. Two men stood guard, to keep out malcontents as well as those who weren't yet old enough to provide for the Darkers.

People like her, on both counts.

But a few days ago she had approached these two guards outside of the Darker mealtimes. In exchange for a few kisses and some prolonged groping beneath her shirt, they had agreed to let her witness today's morning feed. A few minutes earlier they had swept the tunnel near the gates, clearing out other lurkers, but letting her stay. So she knew the deal still stood.

She peered through the hatch.

The room was filled with light, for the feeding had already begun. And the gruesome scene laid bare by the light horrified her.

The Feeding Room was cavernous, and bare of any furnishing or decoration. During each feeding, thousands upon thousands of times over the years, the plating of the walls, floor and ceiling had been slagged to liquid only to cool and re-solidify, so that the boundary of the room was amorphous and changed by the day. The underlying pipes and ductwork of the infrastructure were exposed in various places, themselves half-melted and twisted out of shape.

The Feeding Room had obviously not been constructed with its present function in mind. Which begged the question: what *was* its original function? Did it even matter?

No, at that moment, it did not matter to Embra.

Her mother had died in this very room, after a Darker had fed too deeply upon her.

For her, the horror of the feeding overrode all other considerations. Her eyes roved from one point to another, the horror growing with each passing moment.

The room was occupied by a mixture of Darkers and Flamers. The Flamers were ordinary humans like Embra herself. Even though there were about five hundred in the Pen, there were only about ten of them present in the Feeding Room that morning, since they only flamed every two weeks like clockwork. But the Darkers...

The Darkers!

They infused her with a sense of disgust every time she beheld them.

They were tall, far taller than Embra's people. So tall that they would have to crouch to move through the tunnels. Which meant they didn't belong here, Embra realized. The catacombs weren't made for them.

They were bone-thin, gaunt, emaciated. Flesh the color of old parchment sagged over the bumps of ribs, hips, bones, tendons, muscles. Cheekbones and chin were sharp points. The nose was just two holes in the skin of the flattened face. The mouths lipless, the teeth serrated and crooked, like bits of broken ceramic jammed into the jawbone. Their hands and feet were clawed, their long sharp nails chipped. Their membranous wings, enormous when fully extended, were kept folded behind their backs when inside the tunnels. Their small eyes were strange: lidless ovals, black near the nose holes, transitioning to flame red at the outer edge.

Like Embra's people, they were a race divided into two sexes. The males each had a thin, rope-like organ dangling from naked loins, while the females were distinguished by flattened, dangling breasts like empty sacks of dried parchment.

For Embra, overlaying their repulsive visual appearance was that disconcerting sense of emptiness, of a hungry, sucking absence leading to some dark place outside the universe.

What Embra saw was repeated many times across the vast space of the Feeding Room: one of her people would suddenly jolt and throw their arms wide as if transfixed, and then burst into flame, swallowed within spheres of blinding light that wavered from red to blue to orange to white, cycling through the spectrum. Fiery streamers of intensely hot plasma licked across the surface of the small stars of which they had become the fleshly cores.

A few Darkers would step toward one of the flickering conflagrations, snakelike tongues hungrily licking the rims of their lipless mouths. As the Darkers approached, the surface streamers would erupt toward the Darkers as if drawn to them. The closer the Darkers got, the greater the amount of fiery plasma that would leap out and bathe them in white hot fire. The Darkers would eventually step fully into the fire and vanish from sight in the blinding whiteness. Gradually the light would begin to fade, revealing both the Darkers and the Flamer once more. Both races were now transfixed, the Darkers seeming to swell, invigorated, their faces beatific and gasping with joy as they drained and ingested the plasma fire through mouth, nostrils, and leathery skin itself. Correspondingly the Flamer would wither, sagging, skin paling and sinking down onto bone. Finally the Flamer would drop to his or her knees, the light flickering and finally dying, their pent up energy fully expended, at which point the Flamer collapsed face down onto the floor, unconscious, seemingly lifeless.

But Embra knew they weren't lifeless, just considerably weakened. Other Flamers would step from where they had been waiting along the walls, collect the collapsed Flamer and drag him or her from the room, past Embra and the guards and onward, deeper into the Pen toward the recovery room.

Embra knew the flaming was an ordinary occurrence for her kind, part of the normal biological process. What was abnormal, and so horrifying to her, was the way the Darkers fed off such a beautiful part of the Flamer's life, sucking it into that insatiably hungry emptiness within them that apparently only she out of all her people could see. This was sick. It was wrong, it was unnatural. She had, of course, heard about it before, but this was the first time she had witnessed it first hand.

And supposedly there were Feeding Rooms just like this, in other Pens throughout Darker territory. What she was witnessing was just a small fraction of the horror.

"No! This has to stop!" she screamed at the guards. Several nearby Darkers turned to look at her, and her habitual paranoia set in. She raced away from the Feeding Room.

# 02 - Flight

She ran blindly, careless of where she was going. She nearly collided with several people, who leapt out of her way at the last instant. They shook their fists after her, cursing her vigorously and admonishing her to slow down and look where she was going. The gas lamps away from the gates and the Feeding Room were never extinguished, so she couldn't use darkness as an excuse for her carelessness.

Suddenly realizing that she was standing out, she heeded their words and slowed to a walk.

Behind her, she could sense spots of emptiness all clustered in one area: the Feeding Room. Breakfast was still in full swing.

But one spot had detached from the cluster, and seemed to be trailing her far in the distance. Following her? Had her shouted words caught more unwanted attention than she had thought? Enough that they would take her in for questioning?

Such a thing was not unheard of.

She almost panicked and broke into a run again. But she fought the urge. It was also not unheard of for Darkers to occasionally wander the tunnels of the Pen, looking for signs that any malcontents might be joining forces or arming themselves. Or they might wander for other reasons. Some of them actually had friends among the Flamers. Also, she just then realized that her random flight was taking her toward a Well Room. Perhaps the Darker behind her was a supervisor coming to check on the well.

She relaxed again. The odds that she was being pursued were slim.

But not nonexistent.

She passed the Well Room, intending to position herself further up the tunnel where she could watch the door and see whether the Darker behind her entered.

As she passed, she glanced into the room.

It was cylindrical, and cramped, no more than ten paces in diameter. But its height was...Well, Embra didn't know what its height was, but it went all the way up to the surface.

There were no Darkers within, of course. Just her own kind. Just Flamers. Some of them were currently flaming, discharging their plasma into coils, which absorbed it and stored it for later consumption by the Darkers. Uncharged coils lay in a pile near the Flamers, ready for use. The coils were small, just three twists. Cool rods of metal forged by the ancients, twisted into their present shape. Impossible to make nowadays; the Flamers had lost the secret of their manufacture, and the Darkers had never possessed it.

Once a coil had been charged by a Flamer, the brightly glowing, white hot thing was placed into one of the buckets that had been lowered from the opening far above in the ceiling. The opening was not visible from down here, since there were no gas lamps that far up the sides of the cylindrical shaft. Neither was there any light from the surface, since the surface itself had been plunged into an eternal night long ago, when the Darkers had extinguished the Sun. Or so her spotty and perhaps unreliable knowledge of history said.

The constant noise of ratcheting gears and rattling chains as the buckets were raised and lowered was overpowering.

But as she glanced into the room, a full bucket was being sent up to someone far above. The bucket was alive with the light from the coil it contained, and lit the walls of the upper shaft as it ascended. Soon the opening was visible, a tiny oval of blackness in the surrounding rusted metal of the shaft. The bucket wobbled a bit, and then disappeared through the opening, where the coil it contained would eventually be discharged into the hungry emptiness of a Darker living on the surface, a Darker who didn't have the convenience of a readily available Flamer as did the catacomb dwellers.

The surface! She had dreamed of it her whole life. Not much was known about it, for no one in the Pen had ever been there. Just rumors and bits of knowledge passed down through the ages. It was said there were people like herself living up there among the Darkers, people who lacked the Spark and the consequent need to flame. The Ashenfolk, they were called. Were they merely legends, or were they real? That imminence, that potentiality that she could always sense, that she was sensing even now, somewhere up there, within what felt like miles of the top of the well: might it perhaps be one of the Ashenfolk?

All this she took in with a glance as she passed the Well Room. She put the last question out of her mind. The proximity of the Darker was her concern at the moment.

She moved on up the tunnel to an intersection and positioned herself just around the corner, so that she could see back to the Well Room without herself being seen.

Moments later, the Darker turned a far corner and approached the Well Room.

He passed it by without sparing as much as a glance inside.

Panic lit her up again. He *was* after her!

She tensed, leaning forward onto her toes, preparing to flee. Her advantage was that she had lived in the Pen all her fifteen years of life. She knew these tunnels, every nook and cranny. Most of the Darkers only came here once or twice a day, and rarely strayed far from the Feeding Room.

But something held her back. She stayed at the corner, peering around it, watching the Darker. He was having difficulty seeing in the light of the widely-spaced gas lamps, shielding his eyes against it with one clawed hand. It was possible that in his half-blindness he wasn't aware of her watching, and it was still possible that he was only coincidentally heading in her direction.

A hatch along the tunnel wall between Embra and the Darker suddenly opened. An old crone appeared, standing in the opening and peering into the tunnel. The grey-haired old woman stretched and yawned, apparently having just awakened.

Her name was Ieldra. Embra was familiar with her, as she was with most of the inhabitants of this Pen. After all, she had lived in close quarters with all of them for her entire life, and such closeness bred familiarity, if not friendship or intimacy.

Ieldra was a loon, always shuffling around in her threadbare, hole-ridden smock with her dirty wrinkled old legs exposed, and mumbling incoherently to herself and occasionally cackling like the mad woman everyone believed her to be.

The old crone smiled at the Darker as he passed...

...and then she burst into flame. A flame unlike any Embra had ever witnessed. Not that she had witnessed many: flaming was like sex, rarely done in front of children, and a great effort was done to shield them from it.

But Ieldra flamed, a hot, wild, controlled conflagration that reached out like the arm of some brutal monster and engulfed the Darker. It screamed, a shrill, high-pitched shriek of terror so unlike its normal metal-grinding-metal tone. And then it too burst into flame. Rather than consuming the fiery plasma as when it fed, the Darker was itself consumed, flash-burned into molten ash which splattered onto the tunnel wall opposite Ieldra's door and melted into the metal, leaving a black shadow in the outline of the Darker.

Ieldra's flame extinguished. She sagged against the jamb of her hatch, wheezing and gasping for breath.

In the sudden silence, hatches all along the tunnel were opening, and people peered forth to see what the commotion was about. Some of them looked weak and pale; these were the ones who had so recently fed Darkers back in the Feeding Room.

Ieldra straightened, mustering what little strength her frail old body had left in it. "Come," she said to Embra, who had been stunned into immobility by the unexpectedness of the shocking event. She took the young girl's wrist and pulled her into the living space at her back, and closed the hatch upon the curious faces timidly inching closer.

The room was tiny. The only furnishings were an uncomfortable-looking cot in one corner, a rickety table in the center of the room, and along another wall, a second table with a dented steel pitcher and a warped steel plate on the top.

"It's time for you to leave," Ieldra said without preamble.

"What did you do out there?" Embra said.

"What I had to do," Ieldra said. "I saved you. I wound the clock of Destiny, set it to counting down." She began pacing around the room, muttering. "It could have been me, when I was your age. But I was too afraid! I had no one to push me. But you have me, thank all the stars in the sky!"

"What are you talking about?" Embra asked. "What stars? What is 'sky'?"

"You'll find out soon enough."

Ieldra went to the corner of the room opposite the hatch and pulled a section of metal plating from the wall. A dark, rectangular opening stood revealed. "You must leave now. They know what I've done, and they're coming. You can feel them, I know you can."

Embra suddenly became aware of the approach of a multitude of those empty spots, those empty, hungry spots that told her where Darkers were even when she couldn't see them. They had left the Feeding Room and were hurrying this way.

Embra's heart leapt into her throat. "I don't understand any of this! Why did you kill that Darker? You crazy old woman!"

Saying nothing, Ieldra doffed her smock, revealing her wrinkled, pale old flesh, her sagging dugs. She presented her backside to Embra, whose eyes were instantly drawn to the birthmark between the old woman's shoulder blades: wavering flames emanating from a star. "I show you this, which is like your own, so you'll know that you can trust me."

Realization sank in. "You're special like me," Embra said.

"Once, I was," Ieldra replied, putting her smock back on. "Now, no longer. Nature provides a potentially special person once per generation. Once, long ago, that was me. But I didn't fulfill my potential. Now, it is you, and I have lived long enough to make sure you fulfill yours. Perhaps that was my destiny all along."

She thrust Embra toward the dark opening in the wall. "Now go! Hurry! They're almost upon us. Find your way to the surface, and then seek out the Bridge Keeper."

"But why?" Embra said plaintively, refusing to be pushed away. "I don't understand. How did you know about my birthmark? Why are we special?"

"No time!" Ieldra shrieked.

She shoved Embra, this time with a forcefulness that belied her advanced age. Taken off guard and unable to resist, Embra found herself half falling, half scrambling into the opening.

"But I can't just leave!" Embra protested. "At least let me gather a few things from my room." Her room. Her bare, lonely room that wasn't much different from Ieldra's. A room she had once shared with her mother, and earlier still, her father. Both dead now. She really had nothing to go home to, nothing to get. That was just an excuse to avoid leaving the only world she had ever known.

But the Darkers were out in the tunnel now, right outside the hatch.

What am I so afraid of? she wondered to herself. The old woman had killed the Darker, not her.

But despite this, fear and paranoia pushed her deeper into the darkness. She crawled forward on her hands and knees, deeper into some sort of narrow ductwork behind the tunnel walls.

Behind her, Ieldra put the panel back onto the wall, cutting off the gas light, and Embra heard screws turning in the sudden pitch blackness.

And forward she crawled, fleeing the Darkers behind her, not knowing where the ductwork led, unable to see anything at all. No food or water, nothing in her possession other than the clothing she wore, and no idea how to exit the ductwork.

The surface, she thought. How do I get to the surface? And where do I go once I'm there?

She began sobbing as she crawled.

The ducts were narrow and constricting. The only way she could move was to wriggle forward like one of the pale worms that sometimes infested the fruits and vegetables her people grew in the water gardens of the Pen. Too much movement and she would hit her head, or bang her elbows or knees. She did that often, each strike a dull thumping sound as the metal yielded and crumpled beneath her.

There was not enough room to turn around even if she had wanted to. And with each passing minute, she increasingly wanted to, which made her sob even harder, because she knew that route was closed to her. She couldn't go back. She was a fugitive.

Several times as she crawled, she scraped over nails or screws, or tacks, or whatever they were; in the darkness she couldn't tell. But the feel of the things cutting her flesh made her scream, and her tears increased. Even though she couldn't see in the darkness, she just *knew* they were cutting her rather than merely scratching. And the sharp things were caked with ancient rust, the threads clogged with mold, mold which discharged spores into her poor young blood with each cut. She was sure of it.

Eventually she simply stopped. She couldn't go on like this, crawling away into the pitch blackness with no idea where she was going, having her flesh shredded bit by bit, death by a thousand cuts. Each inch forward a gamble that she wouldn't crawl over the edge of a precipice.

She stopped, and lay there sobbing. Suddenly realizing how hot it was in the ducts. Sweat soaked her clothing, and stinging rivulets of it ran into her eyes. She continually blinked it away, and kept on blinking, trying to blink away the darkness. But she couldn't.

She couldn't go on, with only a vague idea where she was going.

The surface.

But the surface was up, and so far she had not gone up a single inch.

Her mind cleared, her sobbing stopped.

Thinking was good, she told herself. Think your way out of this. Think your way upward.

And then she realized that she knew precisely where to go. She could sense it even now, like a beacon: that spot of potential far above her, that spot of imminence that had called to her throughout her entire life. If there'd been enough room to lift her arm, she could have pointed straight at it, followed its small movements with her pointing finger. She had always assumed it was on the surface. She would let it be her guide, her beacon.

As soon as she had resolved herself to that course of action, she had an epiphany: the reason she'd always felt that that spot represented potentiality, or imminence, was because it was her destiny. It was waiting on her. Once she reached it, the potential would be actualized; the imminent would enter the present.

Buttressed by her newfound purpose, she started forward once again, free of tears, and carefully this time, feeling her way along, avoiding the nails and screws. Feeling the ceiling of the duct.

And soon she found a square hole in the ceiling. She wriggled her way upward into another duct, one that slanted slightly upward. And then she found another hole in the ceiling, and climbed again.

Of course, she found grilles in the duct as well, grilles which she could have lifted and crawled through. But these were always on the floor of the duct, and were too small for her to fit through. She didn't want to fit through them anyway, since they led downward, and downward meant away from the surface. And most likely they let into tunnels. She was certainly beyond the tunnels of her pen by now, so any tunnels beyond the grilles would be infested with Darkers. As if in confirmation, a slight breeze wafted up through each grille she passed, carrying with it the strong, acrid, necrotic stench of the Darkers.

So she kept to the ducts, and went upward at each opportunity.

In that way, she slowly but surely made her way toward the surface. The imminence, her destiny, grew ever larger within the field of her sight beyond sight.

Then — what must have only been hours after she had fled the Pen, for she was only then beginning to grow hungry — the duct she was wriggling through came to an abrupt end.

She felt around her in the darkness: walls all around except in the direction from which she had come.

"No!" she screamed.

She was just below the surface, she was certain of it. She was practically on the same level as the beacon that had been guiding her. Perhaps only a thin barrier of metal separated her from that mysterious world she had never known: the surface!

She lay on her back and relaxed. She stilled her thoughts, and used the one other ability that set her apart from everyone else she had known: she felt the metal around her. She felt the tiny little things of which it was made. The impossibly small things, in numbers beyond her ability to count, that combined to make the metal.

And she pushed those in the metal above her. She told them to move away.

They did.

Slowly, a corner of the ductwork sheet above her peeled back. And then she encountered a piece of metal beyond that, a big, heavy piece, thick steel, like the wall section which Ieldra had earlier removed from the wall of her room. That piece too peeled back, and a breeze blew through the narrow opening.

Beyond, she felt a large open space.

The surface beckoned to her, and she pulled herself up and out from the duct.

# 03 - Valdrake

Valdrake dragged the old woman into the Throne Room and tossed her face-up onto the floor before the Emperor of the Night.

He knelt, pressing his forehead to the cold metal floor. "Great One," he said.

The Throne Room was vast and elegant, lined with thick steel columns along two walls which formed an aisle up to the dais that supported the throne. Tapestries were hung on the walls, ancient tapestries from the time before they had come to this place. Tapestries made with fibers that had been ripped from the guts of enormous beasts which had lived with them in the dark between the husks of the stars upon which they had once fed. Tapestries depicting the great events in the long history of the Darkers. Tapestries that had once hung not upon walls, but upon the interstellar dust.

What the Throne Room's original function had been no one remembered. But now the cavernous space housed the Emperor of the Night. The only place in the catacombs large enough to contain his enormous bulk and shield him from the eyes of God.

The Throne itself, a gigantic chair fit for the Emperor's massive form, was an ornately carved fragment of the core of a star, brought by their ancestors from the old places. It was said that the Emperor's own great-great-grandfather had single-handedly ingested the star from which the Throne was made. Which was ridiculous, of course. Only God could ingest entire stars by Himself.

The Throne was the only truly dark surface in the entire room. To Valdrake's eyes, everything else — he and the Emperor, the body of the old woman, even the walls themselves — was awash with heat.

Or rather, the Throne was the only truly dark surface save one.

The Emperor leaned forward, lowering his towering head from where it nearly touched the high ceiling.

"What creature is this?" the Emperor asked, gently probing the corpse with one thick, clawed finger.

Valdrake rose from his prostrate position and reached for the heat source upon the floor. A source from which the heat was rapidly fading as the last life fled from her. A shame that she couldn't have been made to flame one final time to feed someone. A waste of precious energy.

He turned her over so that the darkness between her shoulder blades was visible: a sun surrounded by stylized, wavering flames. Or rather, the birthmark was invisible to him. Much like the Throne, to his eyes, she was like a negative: the part of her that should have been blazing — the birthmark, which represented a star, after all — was darkness, while all around it, the rest of her blazed with rapidly dying heat.

The Emperor drew back in shock. "A Flame Queen!" he gasped.

"How can this be, High One?" Valdrake asked. "This trait was purged from the species long ago!"

The Emperor had composed himself. "Obviously not. Where was she found?"

"Pen 322, High One."

"Search the Pen," the Emperor commanded. "She might have had offspring."

Valdrake shook his head. "Not according to the Chief of that Pen. She was a loner, a crazy old woman who never took a mate."

"Perhaps so. Or maybe the Chief is lying."

"There was talk of a girl, Great One."

"Yes?"

"Yes. This old woman murdered one of our own, and was seen taking a girl into her room. The girl was not found when the woman was apprehended."

"Again I say search the Pen," the Emperor commanded. "Find the girl. She's a Queen. Why else would this reclusive old woman have helped her? Strip them all and check them for the mark. Where there was a Queen, there may be Kings."

Valdrake nodded. "Anything else, Great One?"

The Emperor nodded, a mere bubbling of his heat source in the pitch blackness of the room. "Yes. The old one might have passed her time, but this young one is a prime threat. If you can't find the girl in Pen 322, take all the resources you need and scour the world. Find her at all costs. In fact, General, scour the entire world anyway. We need to know if the Flame Kings are still in their blood as well. Were you able to question the old woman before she died?"

Valdrake shook his head. "No. She took her own life just before we reached her."

The Emperor began pacing anxiously, a mere few steps from one side of the room to the other due to his size. "Then we don't know how much the child knows of herself. Put all her Pen-mates to the question. We need to know how much she knows."

Valdrake nodded. "I would also suggest, Great One, that we should assume she knows everything, and send a detachment to wait for her at the Bridge. That is, of course, where she would go if she is self-aware."

The Emperor nodded. "Wise. Do it!"

Valdrake bowed. As he left the Throne Room, he heard the Emperor break the old woman's body, presumably to devour the dying Spark within her.

Let no crumb go to waste.

# 04- World of Darkness

Jordan was awakened, as he was every morning, by the clucking of his chickens. The familiar sound drifted in through the window above his bed, along with a sudden puff of wind that was gone as quickly as it came: the bow shock of the distant Sun passing on its course. He'd learned that in school recently. A sun which he had never seen, but which seemed like it might be a nice thing to behold.

"But what's the Sun for?" he had asked his teacher. A sphere atop a distant, tall shaft that raced around the world in a day, known to the world's inhabitants only by the wind of its passage. What a strange notion!

The four other guys in his class had sighed and slapped their foreheads. "You ask too many questions!" they always told him. Questions to which the teacher rarely knew the answers. Or at least pretended not to. They were tired of his wasting their time on unanswerable questions.

The big Darker woman had shrugged. "I do not know," she predictably replied. "That's just the way the world was made."

Jordan lay in bed for a few minutes longer. The clucking of his chickens grew more insistent. Finally he sat up on the edge of his bed, yawned and stretched, then pulled on his brown burlap pants and his dirty grey burlap shirt. Slipped on his sandals and left his bedroom.

In the living room, he lit the lamps, making sure the wicks were low for a dim light, as his parents would be up and about soon. He could already hear them stirring behind their bedroom door.

Outside the front door, he lit the lantern that was sitting on the bench beside the door. The lantern did little to dispel the pitch blackness of the new day, but it was enough to provide a flickering sphere of light around him.

Picking the lantern up, he went around to the chicken coop at the side of the house. The chickens were so hungry that they had stopped their clucking, and were now pecking at the metal plates of the ground, amazingly enough able to ferret out bits of moss and fungus growing on the rusted steel, mostly around the rivets.

Jordan hung the flickering lantern on a fence post, and then scooped a cupful of feed from the bag by the gate. "Here you go, little chickies," he said, scattering the feed around the enclosure. Instantly the chickens gave up on the fungus and descended upon the feed, jockeying for position with much clucking and flapping of wings.

Once the chickens were fed, he fed himself. He kept a basket of fruit and vegetables on the front porch. It was nearly empty, so he would have to go to his garden sometime today and gather more. He kept a garden a short distance away, in an area he and his parents kept secret, since it was a bona fide dirt garden like the ancients had farmed. Dirt was a rare commodity, and they had a whole twelve square feet of it, a foot deep! Planted with all sorts of nice fungus, moss and other edible, nutritious plants. The garden was where Jordan got most of his food. The garden and his chickens. He didn't know where his parents had gotten the dirt, but they were rich because they possessed it, as long as they were able to keep it secret.

He picked up the last skepple in the basket, rubbed it against his sleeve, then took a bite. The juicy, tart meat razzed his taste buds and left a tingling trail as it slid down his throat.

As he leisurely ate the skepple, he looked the house over. His father had constructed it from metal sheeting he scavenged from a section of ground a few miles away, in an area where the plating was loose and easily removed. In fact, some of the plating had blown away on the wind before his father had found the site, exposing the infrastructure below.

The house looked okay, but then it always did. It was well-built. But his father had him check it every day anyway.

"You need to learn how to keep a house up," Father always said whenever Jordan complained about the seemingly pointless duty.

"Why?" Jordan had said once. "When I come of age, I'm going to live in the catacombs. I won't need a house in the catacombs."

"You're not living down there," his father had instantly replied. "Your kind are only allowed down below if they're in the Pens. And you're an Ashenfolk, so they won't let you in the Pens."

"You don't want to be in the Pens anyway," Mother had said firmly.

"Why not?" he had asked, but she didn't respond.

Jordan finished eating and went inside. Mother and Father were up now, sitting at the table. Mother was knitting a cushion to stick under the thin, sagging bags of her breasts, which had lately begun to chafe her. Father was reading one of his mysterious books which were printed with an ink that was invisible to Jordan's eyes. They were both keeping as far from the dim light as possible.

Father rustled his wings in greeting, and Jordan rubbed his hands in poor imitation. "Good day, Father," he said.

"Are you well today?" Mother asked.

It wasn't their usual morning small talk, but she had been asking him that a lot lately, as if she expected he might not be, or was expecting something to happen and wished to know if it had.

"I'm fine," Jordan responded.

"Will you be going to school today?" she asked.

"Not today, I don't think," he replied.

"Good," she said.

"It feels like a fine day," he said. "Tomar at school thinks it's going to rain today."

Rain. Water falling from the darkness. He wondered where it came from. The stars? He always liked to tend his garden in the rain, make sure his plants caught enough water.

Father looked up from his book. "We're ready to feed," he said pointedly.

Jordan nodded. He grabbed the coil from its place on the table.

"I'll be back shortly," he told them cheerfully, and left on his morning trip to the well.

As he walked, the coil dangled from a belt loop on his backside, flopping around with each step as if alive. He held the lantern at waist level so that he could safely pick his way across the ground. The ground plating was old, and the panels no longer fit flush together the way they must have when the world was new. He'd been this way so many times that his feet had literally worn the metal smooth. But he could still catch a foot on the uneven joints of the ground panels. He had done so more than once just in the past year, sending him sprawling to scrape his face along the rough metal to either side of the path. Once he had even tripped smack down upon a rivet, which had left a permanent, dented scar on his forehead. Then occasionally there were places where the plating had been ripped up entirely, and a trip would mean a nasty fall down among the pipes and ductwork of the infrastructure, probably earning broken limbs or ribs rather than mere scrapes and bruises.

He paused once and held up the lantern as something passed overhead, making a leathery flapping sound. He saw nothing, since the lantern was just a tiny speck of light in the black immensity of the day, and whatever it was had passed by beyond the reach of his light. Of course he knew it was probably a Darker soaring about its business. But he had always been afraid of the dark, and his young imagination peopled it with all sorts of terrifying monsters. Unseen things lurked just beyond the edge of his light, he just knew it. But somehow, over the years, he had come to terms with that. If those unseen things reached out and pulled him away into the black, so be it. There was nothing he could do to prevent it. He just had to avoid their reaching arms, that was all.

As he lowered the lantern to resume his walk to the well, a shooting star passed overhead. There weren't many stars up there in the sky. So few that he could easily count them all if he put his mind to it. A shooting star was a rare thing and shouldn't be wasted. So he quickly made a wish before some other observer out there in the dark beat him to it.

He wished that he lived in a world of light rather than darkness.

As he looked upward at the stars, a drop of water struck his cheek. A portent of the rain Tomar had predicted? He wiped the drop away, wondering if it had fallen all the way from one of the stars up there.

He resumed his walk.

A short time later, he very nearly tripped over a curl in the ground that he was sure had not been there his last trip. The metal panel was twisted upward at one corner, as if something had tried to pull it up. Or had pushed out from underneath. Such a feat would require great strength.

He looked around at the enveloping darkness, fearing the monsters he could not see. Surely only one of them possessed the necessary strength to bend the ground up like this.

Setting the lantern down, he looked under the twisted plating. There was a duct just below, open to the air. He'd never seen open ductwork before; he could just climb down there and go wriggling his way down into the catacombs. He half-considered doing so right then and there. He'd always had a desire to see the underworld. Just a quick trip down, maybe look around a bit, back before his parents even knew he'd gone.

But no. Not this time. They knew how long it took him to go to the well and back, and they were waiting on their breakfast. If he was gone much longer than the usual brief trip, Father might get worried and come looking for him.

His parents had always been overly protective of him. They didn't even like him going to school. But they knew it was necessary for him to socialize with kids of his own kind.

He didn't know why they were so protective of him, but he had always suspected it was one of the reasons they lived out here in the middle of nowhere, rather than within a Darker village, or even a village of the Ashenfolk.

It was unusual for Darkers to raise human children, and both he and his parents were at the best of times frowned upon for it; at the worst of times, the recipients of trouble. If he took the time to explore the duct, they would suspect trouble.

Besides, suppose there *was* a beast lurking out there in the darkness, a beast which had come out of this very duct. Did he really want to climb inside? It might be the beast's lair.

Having thoroughly frightened himself, he picked up the lantern and resumed his trip to the well.

For the rest of the way, he occasionally thought to hear the soft pad of feet somewhere out in the darkness. Each time he caught the sound, he stopped and listened, but heard nothing. If someone was out there, they seemed to be matching his steps, stopping when he stopped, so that he couldn't be sure he was hearing anything at all. Maybe just an echo. But he'd never heard such an echo before. Sure there were hills around, and the occasional metal tree — strange structures of branched pipe that rose from the ground, whose purpose was lost to memory. But the metal of the hills was too corroded and covered with fungus and moss, the trees were too small and rounded, to reflect much sound.

*It's the monsters out there*, he told himself. But they had never made such sound before. If indeed he wasn't actually imagining the footfalls. By the time he neared the well, he had convinced himself that he was just more anxious than usual, and his mind was playing a trick on his ears.

Ten minutes after leaving the house, he reached the well. Of course, he'd been able to see it a few minutes before he reached it. It couldn't be seen from his house, due to the curve of the horizon, but at a certain point along the path, it rose into view like a tiny star in the distance, a beacon of light in the distance shining up into the dark sky, growing larger as he'd approached. The light was plasma fire from below, of course.

The well was a five-foot diameter hole in the ground with a foot-high encircling wall. The wall and the ground were of one piece, an unusually large section of metal plating from which the wall extruded.

Standing upon opposite sides of the wall were two metal girders supporting a rotating axle which spanned the hole. The axle itself had a central sprocket which dragged a chain up from the depths of the well, a chain to which large buckets were attached at regular intervals. A steam engine at the side of the well pistoned noisily along, rotating the axle, which turned the sprocket that rotated the bucket-chain system. Adding to the racket of the engine, the chain rattled and ratcheted as it spun up from the depths and back down, and the buckets clunked when they crested the sprocket and flipped over for the downward journey.

Bates, the old geezer in charge of maintaining the engine and bucket-chain system, was not presently at the well. Jordan rarely saw him, which was fine with him. Bates was a strange one, his mind moving in mental spaces as dark as his stooped old body did.

There was, however, a Darker at the well. Unusually tall with a wickedly sharp talon at the end of each wing bone, this one sported the beginnings of a tail between its saggy buttocks, an unusual feature among Darkers. Jordan recognized him — Blaggath, a reclusive Darker who roosted in a nearby hill whose metal plating had been torn away so that it was just a squarish mound of girders, rebar and piping.

Blaggath, clutching a glowing-white charged coil in his clawed hands, turned from the well and hissed as Jordan approached. With a hateful glare at Jordan, he leapt into the air and flapped away into the darkness toward his house.

Blaggath was one of those who didn't like the idea of Darkers raising Ashenfolk.

Jordan longed to make a rude gesture after the departing Darker bigot. But long years of subservience had bred an instinctive respect for the Darkers into humanity, so he was unable. At least that's what he told himself. It was easier to blame his passive acceptance of Darker scorn on that than on cowardice.

He set the lantern down on the wall, then unfastened the coil from his belt loop and put it into a descending bucket. It usually took about five minutes for a charged coil to be sent up, so he sat down on the wall and waited.

He peered into the well. The light emanating from the well was too bright to see anything down there. Sometimes he wondered how the coils were charged. He supposed when they reached the bottom of the well, the buckets must pass through some sort of pool of fire before they looped back upward. But he didn't know for sure. It was one of those things his teacher didn't seem to know, and neither did his parents.

Once, though, he had heard a rumor from a schoolmate that Flamers lived at the bottom of the wells, and that they discharged themselves into the coils. But that was ridiculous. Everyone knew the Flamers had been wiped out by the Darkers long ago, before the Darkers and humans had made peace.

Then a troubling new thought occurred to him: who was in the Pens that his mother had once said he didn't want to live in? If his kind were only allowed in the catacombs if they lived in the Pens, and Flamers and Ashenfolk were both the same kind, and Ashenfolk weren't allowed in the Pens, then who lived in the Pens? The implications of the question stunned him.

"Hey," someone shouted into his ear.

He jerked in shock, and nearly toppled over into the well.

But someone caught his arm, preventing the fatal plunge.

A girl.

There was a girl standing beside him. The engines and the bucket system were so loud that he hadn't heard her approach.

She was very pretty. A head shorter than he was. Long blond hair that was dirty with oil, long pale arms covered with scratches so recent they hadn't yet scabbed over. And a nice body, judging by the way her stained burlap clothes bulged in all the places he had so recently begun to like in a girl.

She smiled at him. A smile that felt like a light flooding into his soul.

Filled with sudden joy, he smiled back.

She smiled wider, blinding him, then leaned close to shout in his ear, "My name is Embra. I've been following you."

# 05 - At the Well

"You've been following me?" Jordan repeated.

"Yes," Embra responded.

"Since when?"

"I was watching from the darkness when you stopped and looked into the place where I came out of the ground."

"You came out of that duct?" It hadn't been the lair of a monster after all, then. He glanced her over once again. *Definitely* not a monster.

She nodded.

"But why did you come out of the ground?" he asked.

"Because I lived down there."

"In the Pens?" he ventured.

"You know about the Pens?"

"A little," he replied. "So you live there?"

"I did. Up until a few hours ago."

"What are you?" he asked, remembering the troubling thought that had so recently occurred to him, regarding who lived in the Pens.

"What do you mean, what am I?" she asked.

"I mean, are...are you a Flamer?"

She looked uncertain. "I suppose so. I haven't flamed yet, and you can't really know whether you are until you actually do it. But everyone in my Pen was a Flamer, so it's a pretty safe assumption that I am too."

His eyes widened. So it was true! There were still Flamers in the world! It was such wonderful news that he wanted to run through the world screaming it out.

"Are you?" she asked.

He shook his head. "I'm Ashenfolk." He felt ashamed to admit it. But why? What was so embarrassing about not having an active Spark? She and he were both human, after all. Equals. Weren't they?

"But why do you stay in the catacombs?" he asked. "Why not come up here where everybody else lives?"

"Everybody else?" she repeated. "There are surely as many of us down below as there are of you up here. And anyway, I'm up here now, aren't I?"

"Yes, and welcome," he said. "But why don't you all come up here?"

"Because we're prisoners down there!" she said. "We're the food source of the Darkers."

"No!" he said.

"Yes!" she said. "Why do you think I came up here? I escaped."

She pointed at the well behind him. "Your coil is back."

He looked behind him, disoriented by the abrupt change of topic. The bucket was coming back up with his coil inside it. The coil glowed brightly with tongues of plasma fire licking the curves. Carefully, he unclipped the bucket from the chain and set it on the ground. He would need the bucket to safely carry the charged coil back to his parents.

"Who do you think charged that?" she challenged.

"Flamers?" he asked.

She nodded. "Flamers. We're kept in the Pens down there for the convenience of the Darkers. Who's your coil for?"

He hesitated, then said, "My parents."

"Your parents?" she asked, incredulous. "Your parents are Darkers?"

Again he hesitated, then nodded.

"Darkers don't give birth to humans," she said, skeptical.

He rolled his eyes. "Of course not. I'm adopted."

"Why?" she asked.

"Why what?"

"Why would Darkers adopt a human?"

"Kindness?" he asked. "My real parents were killed just after I was born, and my Darker parents took me in because they were good friends with my real parents."

"Is that what they told you?" she asked, smirking.

"Why would they lie to me?" He suddenly felt put upon to defend himself and his parents.

"Why indeed?" she asked, looking at him speculatively.

Then she pointed at the bucket. "Touch the coil."

"What?" he said. "No! It will burn me."

"I doubt it," she said. "Touch it. Please." She smiled at him again.

Damn that smile!

He bent down and touched the charged coil. The plasma flames licked at his hand, but did no damage, caused no pain.

"You're not Ashenfolk," she told him. "That would have burned your hand off if you were. You're a Flamer."

"No!" Even as he said it, he wondered why he was objecting. As if being a Flamer was a horrible thing!

Then he realized that the real reason for his objection was that if what she said was true, he had been lied to his entire life.

"Darkers don't do things out of kindness," she said, and he immediately recalled Blaggath's hateful glare. "Your parents must have adopted you because they knew that one day you'd start flaming, and then they would have a convenient source of food near at hand. You're in a Pen as surely as I was."

"No!" he shouted. Of course, he'd been shouting all along to be heard above the noise of the engine and the chain, so all he actually did was shout louder. "No, you're wrong. You think you've got it all figured out, but you don't. My parents love me. They love me!"

She looked at him with pity. He couldn't believe it. Pity! But she was so beautiful; her eyes were like little stars in the darkness. Those beautiful, kind eyes wouldn't pity him without reason.

"You're the beacon that guided me to the surface, do you know that?" she said. "All my life, I've sensed you up here. Of course, I didn't know it was you until just recently. But down there in the Pens, you were up here, shining above me like a star in my mind, waiting somehow. You were possibility. Potentiality. But now I'm here, and the waiting is over. You have to run away with me. We have a future together."

He shook his head. "No!" he shouted. Backing away from her, he bent and scooped up the bucket. "No! There are no Flamers up here. It's dangerous for you. They say you're all long dead, and they might not like it if you start coming up here. You should go back down where you belong!"

He turned and raced away into the darkness. It wasn't until he was halfway home that he realized he'd left the lantern back at the well. The charged coil was now lighting his path. Had he left the lantern intentionally? he wondered. For her?

Yes, he realized. Because just as she pitied him, he also pitied her. He had left her alone back there with the monsters that lurked in the darkness. But at least he had left her a light to hold them at bay.

EMBRA WATCHED HIM AS he faded away into the surrounding darkness.

That certainly could have gone better.

When she had crawled out of the duct and into the wide open space of the surface — wide open but an utter mystery to her since she couldn't see much further than her own nose — she had felt so utterly alone and frail in that vast darkness.

She had waited a short time after emerging, thinking that after a while her eyes might be able to make out the lay of the land using light from the stars. But that light was apparently just too paltry, the stars too few, to provide any significant illumination to this mysterious new world. Because even after what felt like more than enough time, she still couldn't see a thing. The darkness was absolute.

Well, not quite absolute: scattered around her in what she figured must be the far distance, were smears of dim, fuzzy light, which she figured must be from villages or other outposts of civilization.

Those distant light sources had given her hope. Apparently the Ashenfolk were not legends after all.

She supposed they could be Darker villages and towns, but she doubted it. The Darkers wouldn't use enough light to be visible from great distances. Assuming those lights *were* at great distances. She wouldn't know for sure until she went to them. And go to them she would, since her best hope for survival was among her own kind.

Not knowing what else to do, she had begun crawling off into the darkness, toward one of those distant patches of light. Crawling because she hadn't felt safe enough to walk upright. Too exposed, visible to any Darkers who might be around. And she had no doubt there *were* Darkers around. Not only that, walking upright would cause greater injury when she tripped and fell, which she had no doubt she eventually would, given that the ground plates were rough, the edges uneven.

Then, not too far from the duct out of which she had crawled, she had stopped. Her tentative plan had been to seek out the distant lights. Then, equipped with a light source of her own, she would go to the beacon which had guided her to the surface. That point of imminence, of potentiality, that always beckoned to her. She could feel it even now, somewhere off to her left.

But now, it seemed she wouldn't have to go to it. For it seemed that it was now coming toward her. She could feel it growing, intensifying, heading her way.

So she had waited in the darkness. And then the guy with the lantern had come along. He had stopped not far from her at all, at her exit from the catacombs. She had watched him, longing to rush out and introduce herself. She had never imagined that the thing she had been sensing her whole life might turn out to be a human like her. And a cute one at that, roughly her own age.

But prudence and habitual paranoia had held her back. She had followed him to the well, walking just beyond the light, stopping when he stopped, observing him.

She was astonished when he reached the hole in the ground and watched him put a coil into a bucket. She felt certain this was the very well she had looked into earlier that morning. She'd seen it from the bottom, and now she was seeing it from the top. The trail he followed was well worn. She wondered if this trip to the well was a daily routine for him.

Incredible. She had been so close to him her entire life, but had never known, separated by an impassable barrier. Well, not impassable, for she had just passed it. Their lives were about to merge, just as Destiny had always intended. Watching him hang back from the well as the Darker who was already there finished his business, she had felt that sense of imminence that emanated from him change, in the same way that the future becomes the present.

The Darker had flapped away into the night, and then she had stepped forward.

"Hey," she had said into his ear, feeling more happiness than she ever had before.

And now he had spurned her and vanished into the eternal darkness.

She looked at the lantern shining brightly on the ground by her feet. Picking it up, she followed after him. He could run, but she would always know where he was. He could never hide from her.

This time, though, she would hang back until he was ready for her.

# 06 - The Parents Feed

By the time Jordan reached home, he was feeling hot. Not hot from anger — he could never be angry at a girl with eyes like Embra's — but physically hot.

What's she done to me? he wondered as he stepped up onto the porch and reached for the door handle. Maybe she had brought something up from the Pens with her. Some sort of sickness that he was now catching.

He entered the house.

His parents had turned off the gas lamps in his absence. But upon his entry, they were fired back up to a tolerably dim level. His father stood by the wall with his clawed hand on the gas regulator. Mother was already sitting at the table in expectation of his return. Father joined her, and Jordan set the bucket on the table between them.

"What took you so long?" his father commented. "I'm starving." Father had already begun drawing plasma streamers from the coil. A fiery blue one curled like a tendril of smoke into his nose, while a fiery red one twisted into his mouth, pulsing like an angry snake.

Mother had not yet begun to ingest her portion. Instead, she looked up at Jordan with concern on her devilish features.

"Are you all right, Jordan? You do not look well. You're sweating, dear."

He wondered if her concern was genuine, or a sham. And then he realized that Embra had indeed infected him with something: suspicion.

"No," he said, wiping his forehead. "I don't feel well."

His father looked up. "Really?" he asked — hopefully?

"I think I'll go lie down," Jordan told them, and went into his bedroom.

For ten minutes he tossed and turned, feeling increasingly hot and uncomfortable. Sweat rolled off him in rivulets, drenching his bed sheets.

Finally, some sort of intuition told him to get out of the house. He leapt out of bed and raced to the front door, startling his parents as he threw it open and jumped out into the darkness.

No sooner had he gotten outside and a safe distance from the house, every pore on his skin opened wide, along with his nose, mouth, and every other available orifice — and he erupted like a volcano. He had a sensation of something flooding out of his body and then igniting, engulfing him in a ball of boiling hot flame and plasma that licked his body and sent jagged tongues of fire lashing out into the darkness. He felt like some hole had opened up deep inside the core of him and sent beams of light and energy sizzling away into the wide, dark universe. He screamed, but it came out as a roar of fire.

He felt he might go on burning forever. But something was draining him. He felt the energy leaking away from him, passing into some hungry void that could take more than he could possibly give.

The pressure lessened, the flames died out. The gates deep within him swung shut, and the night was dark once more.

By the light shining forth from the open door of his home, he saw his parent standing near him, gasping and shivering with ecstasy.

And he knew: they had just fed upon him. Embra was right.

But the part of him that loved his parents shouted, No! They had just helped him! He might have gone on flaming forever if they hadn't been there to draw off the fire. They had raised him, they loved him, and if they had just helped him through a difficult event, if they received nourishment from it, so what? Should the energy have just been wasted, discharged into the cold universe to no purpose at all? And anyway, they could feed whether he was there or not. They didn't need him to feed. Didn't they get energy from the well every day?

Energy from coils charged by Flamers being held prisoner in the Pens down below, a small voice inside him said.

I'm a Flamer, another part of him said. I'm not Ashenfolk. I'm a Flamer!

Embra had been right about that. What if she had been right about everything?

He looked at his parents. Mother was looking at him with pity and remorse, while Father looked at him with — what was that look? Greed? Avarice? Pride? Calculation?

How much did he really know about the workings of the Darker mind? How could he dare imagine that he could correctly read emotions born in alien minds and displayed upon alien faces?

He looked back at them, hoping his face was as inscrutable to them as he was now beginning to believe theirs were to him.

What should he do now? What *could* he do now?

He looked down at his feet. The ground around him had melted, the metal partially turned to slag, which was now cooling back to solidity. Fortunately his flaming hadn't damaged the house; he had gotten far enough away.

His shoes and clothing had burned away, and he stood naked and shivering in the cold darkness. He stepped out of the imprints his feet had left in the metal, and headed for the front door.

"I'm going to lie down," he mumbled to his parents. He was unable to meet their eyes. "I need to rest for a while."

"Of course, dear," his mother said.

He went back to his bedroom, threw on a shirt and pants, and lay down again.

What he really needed to do was think. About everything.

Was he in any immediate danger? He didn't believe so. Assuming Embra was right, they wouldn't harm him, since they needed him to feed off of. Assuming he himself was right, they loved him and would not hurt him. Either way, he could probably stay here safely, indefinitely. So nothing had changed, really, other than that he now felt that he had been betrayed, and that the life he thought he had been living here had been a complete sham. Now the sham was up. But that didn't mean he had to leave or was in danger.

But what about Embra? She obviously thought he needed to flee. But why should he? He wasn't in any danger that he could see. She was the one on the run, not him. Besides, he had left her in the darkness and told her to go home. More than likely, he would never see her again.

That thought made him sad. He suddenly realized that he really did want to see her again. Imagine going through life without ever again seeing the sun of her smile, or those eyes...

He had been lying there for about half an hour when he heard a knock on the front door, and then voices in the living room.

He jumped to his feet. Might it be Embra? Had she found her way to his house?

Cocking an ear, he listened. No. Although he couldn't make out what they were saying, the muffled voices coming from the other room were those of his parents and some other Darker. No, several other Darkers.

He crept to the door and pressed an ear to it.

"We've come for the boy," said an unfamiliar Darker voice.

"You cannot have him," said the voice of his father. "You were well paid for him."

"He's got to come back to the Pens," said the first voice. "The Emperor's cracking down. Our hides will be roasted if he finds out we've been placing Flamers with surface dwellers. Go get him."

"We have more dirt," came his mother's desperate voice. "Pounds and pounds. Leave us alone. We'll bring you pounds of dirt. More than before."

"I can't, it's too risky."

With each word, Jordan's spirits sank. Embra had been so very right, so very terribly right. He was nothing to them. His parents had bought him like some sort of slave. How naive he had been! How simple-minded!

And now the Emperor's soldiers were here to take him back. To the Pens.

Then he considered. He had come from the Pens? It was possible. He had lived with these Darkers since very early childhood. He could not remember a life before them.

But why did the soldiers want him back?

"We're also looking for a girl," said the first voice. "She's a Flame Queen. Her existence has greatly upset the Emperor. Has a strange girl passed through recently?"

"No," said his father.

"No," said his mother.

"Has the boy mentioned anyone?" asked the first voice.

There was silence, perhaps his parents shaking their heads. He had not mentioned his encounter at the well, so there was no reason for them to tell the strange Darker that he had.

"We need to check the boy, make sure he's not a Flame King, and take him back."

Jordan's mind was racing. He needed to get out of here before they stopped talking and actually came back here for him.

He looked at the window above his bed. Too small to escape through.

Desperately he looked around the room. His bed, his dresser, his few paltry possessions. The metal walls.

The only way out was through the door, and that way led to his capture.

He heard a wrenching, twisting sound to his right. He looked over.

A section of the wall beside his bed was bending inward, exposing a triangular opening leading into the darkness outside.

Embra's face appeared in the opening.

"Come on!" she said.

Clawed footfalls sounded in the hallway just beyond his door.

Jordan darted for the opening, threw himself to the ground, and slid through it.

Behind him, he heard the bedroom door bang open.

He took Embra's hand, and together they raced away into the pitch blackness of mid-morning.

# 07 - Hiding

After following Jordan home, Embra hid behind a nearby rise in the ground, like a frozen wave in the midst of a sea of metal, and extinguished the lantern. She settled in to observe, and to wait. Wait for what, she wasn't certain, and she didn't know how long she could do so, because she was growing increasingly hungry with each passing moment. But wait she would, until the time felt right.

When she saw him come running outside and burst into flame, lighting up the entire area, she didn't think the time felt right.

"Try denying you're a Flamer now," she whispered triumphantly. But he was a beautiful star, and she basked in his radiance. She longed for the day when she finally flamed for the first time.

When his Darker parents came out and began feeding on his flames, she still didn't think the time felt right, as disgusting as she found their parasitic behavior. Feeding was rarely fatal, her mother being one of the exceptions.

But when the trio of Darkers came flapping in from the inky blackness and alighted on the front porch of Jordan's ramshackle little metal house, she finally knew the time was right.

She could sense Jordan in the back of the house. After the Darkers had been invited inside, she left the shelter of her small wavy hill and stumbled through the dark toward his house, guided solely by her mental sense of his whereabouts. Lighting the lantern would have been too dangerous.

She smacked face-first into the side of his house before she realized she had arrived. She rebounded backward. Then she lowered herself to the ground, feeling along the wall until she was perpendicular to him. Then, as she had before, she reached out to the tiny parts of the metal and told them to move away from her.

A corner of the metal wall plating in front of her creaked and moaned as it slowly bent inward. Light from Jordan's room leaked outward.

She stuck her face into the opening and saw him standing by the door, looking at her with wide eyes.

"Come on!" she urged him.

He came sliding out through the opening. Both of them stood. He took her by the hand and pulled her after him as he ran away into the darkness.

Ordinarily she would have fought him. She would not be forcefully dragged after some boy! But in this case, she acquiesced and let him lead. He knew the lay of the land, after all, and they were running blindly through the darkness. Well, *she* was, at any rate. According to her theory, *he* at least had some idea of where they were going and what obstacles lay in their path.

The lantern was heavy in her right hand, and she fought the urge to turn the switch that would strike the flint and ignite the gas. The lantern's light might prevent them from tripping and getting hurt, but it would also tell the pursuing Darkers exactly where they were.

And she had no doubt the Darkers *would* pursue. Quite soon, if not already.

"They can see our heat," Jordan panted. "Our only hope is to get over the curve of the horizon as fast as possible."

"Really?" she panted. She had not known that about them.

"Stop for a minute," she whispered to Jordan.

He didn't question her, which was good, as far as she was concerned. She wasn't about to let him take the lead in their relationship. She shook off his hand on her left wrist, and with both hands free, she twisted the lantern's knob several times. The lantern clicked each time, and finally the gas caught on the third attempt.

It didn't matter whether they were over the horizon or not, since the Darkers could see them whether the lantern was burning or not. Might as well use it.

She thrust the lantern into Jordan's hand. "Go. This is your territory."

He nodded and took off. She leapt into motion almost on his heels.

They ran for all they were worth. Not the same path they had followed to the well, she could tell, for that path had been worn smooth by long use. This time they fled along no path that she could see. As far as she could tell, they were simply running aimlessly.

"You *do* have a destination in mind, don't you?" she finally asked when uncertainty had gotten the best of her.

"Oh, yes," he said. "Trust me."

She supposed she did trust him — she had little choice — but trust came hard to her. And it came even harder when she expected to hear the flapping of wings above her at any minute, and the pain of claws closing around her arms, lifting her into the air. She had never seen Darkers fly before, since in the tunnels of the catacombs flight would have been impossible. But she had already seen them flying several times since her arrival on the surface. And it was a terrifying thing to behold, their leathery wings spread out wide, each slow, majestic stroke propelling their skeletal forms through the air.

Soon they came to a wide area of ground where the plating had been torn up, perhaps by the wind, perhaps by something else. Sections of it were scattered on the ground around the gaping wound in the world. Some were bent and twisted, some were rusted through with holes, others were leaning against the few metal trees that dotted the area.

Embra thought the trees were interesting. Perpendicular metal trunks with a few horizontal rods branching off. There were none down in the catacombs. What was their function?

"This is where my father scavenged the material to build our house," Jordan explained. "Some of this mess is his doing, but mostly it was already like this."

He went to the edge of the squarish hole, stood on the lip looking down into the exposed infrastructure. He set the lantern on the ground, then climbed down onto a thick pipe, and reached up to help her down.

"We'd better hurry," he said. "I don't know about you, but I'm more scared than I've ever been in my entire life."

"That's not very encouraging," she scolded as she took his hand and used it to balance herself as she stepped down onto the pipe beside him. Once down, he placed a gentle hand on her waist to help steady her, but she brushed him off.

He shrugged and reached up, grabbed the lantern from the lip of the hole.

"Let's go down a bit more to be safe," he said.

They clambered down past a duct that extended from one side of the hole to the other, appearing from deep back in the darkness among a tangle of girders and pipes and disappearing into the same across the way. Just below that was a long pipe-like structure constructed from girders and metal plating.

"The outside of a tunnel," he told her.

"Really?" she said, looking at it in awe. She wondered if she had ever passed through that very tunnel. Probably not. Her Pen was probably deeper down, and was only a small part of the vast catacombs anyway. So it was unlikely. "You seem to know a lot about the catacombs."

"Not really," he said, sitting down on one of the girders that comprised the tunnel's framework. "I've always been fascinated with them, but I've never been down."

"Believe me, you don't want to go into the catacombs." She seated herself beside him.

"That's what my mother said."

She grunted noncommittally. Then: "Do you think we're safe? Did they see us and follow?"

"I hope not," he said, and she frowned. Perhaps realizing he should be a bit more positive, he continued, "But they probably would have been on us by now if they had. If we made it this far without being seen, we should be safe for now."

He took her hand and pressed it against a large pipe that ran parallel to the girder. It was hot to the touch, and she jerked her hand away.

"The heat should hide us," he told her. "As long as they don't look too closely, any Darkers flying overhead should only see what they expect to see: the heat of the infrastructure."

"What if they're not flying?" she asked, hating the tremble in her voice. "What if they're on foot, and stand at the edge looking down at us?"

"In that case, scream real loud," he said. Then, smoothly and without hesitation this time, as if he were learning how to encourage her, he said, "But they won't be on foot. Darkers fly up here on the surface. They may walk where you're from, but not here. And anyway, there's a wide area to search. If they didn't see us, they don't know where we are. We could be anywhere, and the size of anywhere grows with each passing minute."

She reached out and extinguished the lantern, plunging them into utter darkness.

"Good idea," he said.

"How long should we stay here?" she asked.

"I don't know," he replied.

They sat in silence for a time, listening for the telltale flap of wings in the darkness.

"I'm hungry," she said eventually.

He turned the lantern back on. Sprawling out onto his stomach, he levered himself over the edge of the girder and looked beneath it. He broke something loose, then came back into sitting position with a big piece of fungus in his hands. He held it close to the light, examining it carefully. Then he broke off a piece and handed it to her.

"See if this will hold you over for now," he said.

"Are you sure it's edible?" she asked.

He popped the piece still in his hand into his mouth and smiled at her. "I'm hungry too," he said as he chewed.

With great reservations but no other choice, she put the fuzzy black thing into her mouth and chewed slowly. At first she winced with each bite, but soon realized there was no need. "It's actually quite good," she said.

"You're a strange one," he said.

"You have no idea," she replied.

"It was all I could do not to spit the stuff out."

"Yes, I've noticed you have a bit of a weak constitution." She grinned at him.

He grinned back, then turned off the lantern, and they sat in silence again.

Eventually he asked, "What are your plans? Where do we go next?"

"Then you've decided to join me?" she asked.

"They were going to take me to the Pens," he said. "Or if I turned out to be something called a Flame King, I got the impression there was a worse fate in store for me. From now on, I think I need to avoid Darkers. Even my parents. Which means I can't go home. So where do we go next?"

"To the Bridge," she said.

"What bridge?" he asked.

"I don't know," she said. "Whichever bridge has a bridge keeper. The old woman who helped me escape said I needed to see the Bridge Keeper, so I assume wherever I'll find him, that's the Bridge we're looking for."

"Why do you need to see this Bridge Keeper?"

"I don't know. I assume I'll learn that when I meet him. Do you have any idea how we should go about doing that?" She liked saying 'we.' The thought that she was not alone in this, whatever this was, was comforting.

"Well, you said you found me because you've always known I was there. Is it possible you might find the Bridge in the same way?"

His suggestion was so completely obvious that she wondered why she hadn't thought of it. She was so overcome with the joy of revelation that she reached out and hugged him tightly. As she rocked against him, purring with delight, she reached out with that strange sense that she alone seemed to possess. And there it was: the distant moving point which circled her once per day. Well, not really circling *her*, she realized. But close enough.

It was currently stopped. Why was it stopped? Would it stop again? Had she ever before noticed that it stopped? Or was this even the circling thing? Maybe it was something else. But if so...where was the circling thing? She couldn't sense it anywhere.

As if in answer, the thing she was sensing lurched into motion, picking up speed. Circling once again.

She pulled back from Jordan. "There," she said, pointing straight at the circling point she could not see. And of course, he could not see her pointing in the darkness. "There's something circling. That's where we're going."

"The Sun is circling," he said.

"The Sun?" she asked dumbly. "What is the Sun?"

Jordan explained the Sun to her. "It circles the planet once a day," he said. "It's a black ball that sits atop a tall shaft that pivots around the center of the planet. It's one of the most incredible features of the world."

"Really?" Embra asked. "What is its purpose?"

In the darkness, she felt him shrug. "I don't know. My teacher wouldn't or couldn't tell us."

"Your teacher was a Darker, I assume?"

"Yes."

"Then there's something they're hiding from us," she said. "The Sun is important, even though we don't know why. It may be the most important thing ever. And we need to go there. It may lead us to the Bridge."

"To the Sun it is, then," he said. "But if they're hunting for us, we need to get among other humans as quickly as possible, so we can get lost in the crowd. First, then, we need to go to a city."

"Where is the nearest one?"

"The nearest human city is Pelis," he said. "Thirty miles that way."

What he didn't say, and she silently thanked him for omitting the pessimistic truth they both knew, was that until they reached the city they would be completely vulnerable and exposed to any searching Darker as they crossed an empty wasteland, a crossing that would most likely end in failure.

She turned on the lantern so she could see where he was pointing.

"I've never been there," he said. "But I know we're going to need money. Therefore, we need to get some dirt from my garden. And fast, before my parents think to look for me there. I doubt they would tell the guards about it, because the dirt is worth too much and they wouldn't want the guards stealing it."

Embra was about to ask how he had come by his dirt, for she knew what a rare and valuable thing it was. But before she could speak, a voice called down, "Ho, there! An old man just happens to be passing by and what does he hear? Voices! And he sees a light flicking on and off and on where none should be. What are you young folk doing down there?"

They both looked up to see a hunched-over old man standing on the lip of the hole at the edge of the lantern's light.

# 08 - The Garden

Jordan thought he recognized the old man. "Delvin?" he asked, because due to the dim lighting he couldn't be entirely sure.

"Hello, Jordan," Delvin said.

"You know him?" Embra whispered. She had crouched into a defensive posture, and looked ready to spring up at him.

"Yes," Jordan said. "Relax. He's harmless."

"Oh, harmless, am I now?" Delvin said, and laughed heartily. "You just put old Delvin in a roomful of nubile young women and we'll see just how harmless he is."

"Who is he?" Embra asked.

"He charges coils at the wells and delivers them to various Darkers around the area," Jordan explained.

"He does indeed," Delvin said. "He's got a route, old Delvin does. But do Jordan's parents let him deliver their coils? No!"

"My parents wanted me to charge the coils each day," Jordan continued explaining. "They thought it would help teach me responsibility."

"Responsibility for feeding them," Embra said. "Getting you used to the idea so that when you flamed, you would slip right into your new role. They were grooming you. Oh, they're very cunning, your parents."

Jordan frowned. "Stop talking about my parents like that! They loved me!"

"Tell me you don't still believe that."

His mouth worked, and he glared at her, but said nothing.

"Did old Delvin hear right?" Delvin asked. "You'll be heading for Pelis?"

"You were eavesdropping!" Embra hissed up at him. "How much did you overhear?"

"Enough to know that I may be able to help you," Delvin said. "Listen, young one. Last night I had a dream that I should load my wagon with charged coils and take them to Pelis to sell at market. So I did, and now I'm on my way. It would be a simple matter to slip you under the coils in my wagon."

"The heat from the coils would mask us from any Darker search parties," Jordan told Embra.

"I thought you said Pelis was a human city," she said to Jordan. "Why would he take coils to Pelis? Who there would need them?"

"Mostly it is a human city," he said. "But there are Darkers everywhere, even in Pelis."

She looked up at the old man, still contentious and suspicious. "So a dream just happened to tell you to go to Pelis, and you just happened to travel right past us, and overhear enough to know you could help us."

"What are you implying?" Jordan asked her.

"He could be a spy!" Embra said. "He's working for the Darkers!"

The old man pulled back as if he'd been slapped. "Never!" He looked down at them and held out a hand. "Nothing happens by accident, Embra. Please, let me help."

She glared at him for a moment longer, then softened. She took his hand and he helped her out of the infrastructure. Jordan followed.

Delvin led them to a wooden wagon parked a short distance away. It had great circular wheels, a large bed, and a wide bench for the driver and a passenger or two. The bed was filled to brimming with charged coils, a great, glowing, flaming mass of them that lit the area for dozens of feet around them, providing enough illumination for Embra to finally get a good look at everything. In the harness was an immense four-legged beast, black as the eternal night around them, with sinewy muscles bulging beneath its glistening skin. A long neck with a thick mane of grey hair supported a head with a long snout and eyes as big as plates to let in as much light as possible. Jordan informed Embra that it was called a *mokk*.

Delvin himself was old and stooped over. He walked with the aid of a wooden staff. He was dressed in a brown burlap robe tied at the waist with a fraying rope. His long hair was silver, and the flesh of his face and hands was mottled with liver spots.

Delvin motioned Embra and Jordan around to the bed of the wagon.

"We could just crawl under them," Jordan whispered to Embra, beginning to move coils aside to make room. He still couldn't quite get used to the idea that he could touch them without being burned, and he hesitated slightly before moving each one.

She nodded. "Any Darkers passing overhead wouldn't see us. They would only see the heat from these coils."

"And they probably won't stop to check Delvin, since he's known in the area," Jordan continued. "He probably even delivers coils to some of the Darkers who would be drafted into the search."

"And we wouldn't have to walk to Pelis," she said in relief. Then she sobered. "But this is too good to be true."

Jordan grabbed the rim of the wagon bed, preparing to climb into the wagon. "Is it too good to be true, or is it destiny?"

Suddenly Delvin's staff came cracking down upon the rim of the wagon near Jordan's hands. Jordan leapt back, startled.

"Not so fast," Delvin said. "I seem to recall talk of dirt."

"I knew it!" Embra said. "You old scoundrel!"

"Wanting to be paid for his aid does not make Delvin a scoundrel," Delvin said. "The dream that commanded him to go to Pelis did not command him to aid you. It told him nothing about you. The dream simply said that going to Pelis today would make him rich." He winked at Jordan. "So what do you say, young Jordan? Will Delvin become rich today?"

Jordan wondered what would happen if he said no. Would the old man betray them to the Darkers?

He looked at Embra. "We need to go to the garden for food and money – dirt – anyway. I'll never need the garden again, so he might as well have it."

She nodded reluctantly.

To Delvin, he said, "We'll need to get there fast. As you must have overheard, the garden may be the first place my parents go to look for me. *If* they look for me."

Delvin nodded. "Let us leave at once, then."

Embra burrowed her way into the pile of charged coils. Jordan climbed in after her, and positioned himself up by the driver's bench with his head sticking above the coils so that he would have a clear view of where they were going. Delvin climbed into the driver's seat, picked up the reigns, and shouted a command at the beast in the harness. The *mokk* leaned into the harness, and the wagon lurched into motion.

The wagon trundled across the sprawling wasteland of metal. The rhythmic clip-clopping of the beast's hooves was loud and echoed hollowly in the vast open darkness. Jordan occasionally told Delvin to steer left or right, or around a hill, as required. Once again they followed no visible path; Jordan always approached the garden from a different angle, so as not to wear a path into the metal ground that would alert others that there was something out here.

As they rode along, it began to rain. A soft, warm rain, not a deluge as occasionally pounded the metal plains. The falling water hissed and sizzled as it struck the coils, vaporizing before it had a chance to trickle down through the mass to wet the clothes of Jordan and Embra. Delvin, however, was getting wet, and he grumbled as he worked the reins.

Then a Darker flapped slowly past overhead. But either it wasn't part of any search for him and Embra, or it didn't find anything suspicious about the wagon, because it simply continued on course until it faded back into the darkness.

Ten minutes after leaving the opening in the infrastructure, Jordan had Delvin bring the wagon to a halt.

Embra popped her head up from the coils and looked around, as did Delvin.

"There's nothing here," Embra said in mystification.

Jordan climbed from the wagon, and walked three paces to the right. Bending over, he grabbed the edge of a section of metal plating that looked no different than the others around it. He lifted it, revealing an opening that was mostly dark, but a grayish dark suffused with dim light.

He dragged the metal panel to the left and lowered it to the ground. "Come on," Jordan said, motioning for them to follow. And he climbed down into the opening.

When Embra had climbed from the wagon and down into the opening, she found herself in a dark, narrow tunnel. Light was shining from around a bend a short distance away.

She reached up to help Delvin clamber down into the tunnel, which he did quite adroitly, considering his age and his stooped posture. Maybe that was just an act?

Once he was firmly on the tunnel floor, she went down the tunnel, turned the bend...

...and found herself looking into a room filled with plants.

"Great Bejebus!" Delvin exclaimed as he joined her on the threshold.

There were skepples ripe and ready for the picking hanging from a large bush in one corner. There was a row of maize next to a row of dashberry vines. There were rows of kerrits and potatoes, white beans and soy beans and dafrique beans, and a section of wheat. Celery stalks and mushrooms growing in a rotting stump. All of them had their roots in a layer of rich black soil that covered the entire floor of the room.

"This is a fortune in dirt!" Delvin said.

The sound of the raindrops striking the metal plates of the ground above was loud and constant. Rain water dripped from the ceiling, having trickled down from the surface. It dripped everywhere, pattering softly down upon leaves and fronds and petals and dirt. The sound was pleasant and relaxing.

And hanging from the ceiling at the end of a copper wire, pouring its life-giving light down over all, was a charged coil. This one had lost most of its charge, and Jordan had planned to replace it today, when he came to the garden.

That plan suddenly seemed very far away, part of a different life, someone else's life perhaps. He was a fugitive now, and this might be the last time he saw this garden, his garden, this secret place that had been a home away from home for his entire childhood, this secret place known only to himself and his parents.

His parents.

"We should hurry," he said. "My parents obviously aren't here now, but they could come at any minute. I don't think I should see them again." His throat suddenly felt dry and choked. "If I did, I might want to stay."

Embra laid a comforting hand on his shoulder, and looked at him with that pity in her eyes again.

He pulled away from her, and picked up a large plastic bag from a rack of shelves along the wall. He began filling it with a few skepples, some carrots, a potato, and several handfuls of dashberries.

"Take all the soil you can carry, I guess," he told Delvin. "If you can remember where this place is, I suppose you could come back for more later. But my parents might take exception to that."

Delvin nodded, picked up a bag, and began scooping handfuls of dirt into it.

Jordan put his full bag on the floor of the tunnel, then grabbed another bag. As he began picking more fruit, he said to Embra, "Take a couple of smaller bags and fill them with dirt. We can use it to pay our way in the cities."

"Say please," Embra said, smiling politely but obviously deadly serious.

"Please," Jordan said without hesitation or resentment.

She flashed him another smile and bent to scoop dirt into the bags. As she did so, she commented, "You know, down in the Pens, we have gardens too. But ours use water rather than soil. It's called hydroponics."

She looked sidelong at Delvin as she made this confession, wondering if she had revealed too much by speaking of her place of origin. But the old man didn't seem to be listening; he merely clutched his large bags of dirt and gazed at them avariciously, probably dreaming of how he would spend his newfound wealth.

Jordan merely grunted noncommittally, thinking that as far as he was concerned, water would be an inferior substitute for actual soil. Surely anything grown without soil would not taste as good.

Soon they had gathered enough fruit and vegetables to last them for a few days, although the meals would be sparse and definitely leave them longing for more. But the two bags of dirt Embra carried should buy them more satisfactory fare once they reached the cities, as well as provide them with a month's worth of rooming at an inn.

"A what?" Embra asked.

"An inn," Jordan said. "A temporary place to sleep when you're traveling."

"Oh. We didn't have those in the Pens," she said. This time she uttered the word with less fear, and Delvin still didn't appear to take notice.

Soon they had the wagon loaded and the metal section back in place, concealing the entrance to Jordan's garden. He and Embra were once again burrowed deep down among the charged coils. The wagon lurched into motion, and Delvin oriented it toward Pelis.

As they got underway, Jordan heaved a sigh of relief that he had not encountered his parents at the garden. The garden, and his former life along with it, dwindled into the distance behind them, swiftly swallowed by the inky darkness.

# 09 - On the Road

The journey to Pelis was long and rough. As everywhere else Jordan had seen, the terrain was overall gently curved, but locally uneven, many of the bolts on the ground plates loose and making for a bumpy ride. The wagon bounced and jounced along enveloped in a hemisphere of light that barely held back the overpowering darkness around it. The wheels splashed through puddles of oil or stagnant water or muddy brown sludge or some other viscous liquid. Sometimes the liquid steamed or boiled, sometimes the oil bubbled, sometimes the water was covered with a green scum, or red scum, or black scum.

They passed through clouds of ash that smelled like burning coal raining from the sky; they passed through torrents of rain that smelled like mold and rotting dead flesh; they passed through clouds of hot steam that smelled like the aftermath of a lightning strike belching from holes in the ground.

They passed wells like the one with which Jordan was familiar. They passed a cluster of gigantic cast iron cylinders a hundred feet tall and a hundred across, belching smoke even blacker than the surrounding blackness, roiling columns of smoke dancing with sparks and the occasional tongue of flame that licked upward toward the stars, as if some great fiery beast were slumbering in the depths of the world, ready to unleash a powerful conflagration when it awakened. The odor of sulfur and brimstone lay heavy on this area, and stayed in their lungs for miles beyond.

They passed areas where the ground had been torn up, the plates scattered, exposing the infrastructure, areas just like the one near Jordan's home. In one of these areas, instead of infrastructure, they found a system of enormous interlocking gears lying horizontally, slowly spinning in tandem as they carried out an unknown function as part of some unseen clockwork machine.

They passed rusted metal houses much like Jordan's, some with human families, some with Darker families. In most cases, the residents came out when they heard the clattering of hooves and wheels, and waved as the wagon passed, or glared as it passed, and followed to make sure it passed from their region without making trouble or performing nefarious deeds.

Jordan had never traveled much, and he was astonished to see some of these things. The world was a far gloomier place than he had imagined, and yet filled with more light than he had imagined. Smudges of light were scattered all around on the horizon, marking towns or villages or cities, apparently. Light from the houses they passed. Light from things like the cluster of cylinders they had seen. But everywhere, the light was overpowered by the vast weight of the encroaching darkness. Monsters still lurked just beyond the light; that never changed for him.

Once two Darkers passed by overhead, their underbellies lit up by the light of the charged coils. Their great wings flapped, beating air down upon the wagon, causing the coils to momentarily flare brighter.

They passed away into the darkness, but returned moments later, landing in the wagon's path, forcing Delvin to stop.

Rough questions were asked, about a young human male and a young human female. Delvin gave timid answers, answers that sounded so unconvincing to Jordan's ears that he felt certain the Darkers would search the back of the wagon and find the fugitives.

But the Darkers merely bullied Delvin a bit longer, stole two coils from him, and then flapped away back into the darkness. Jordan and Embra heaved sighs of relief.

The *mokk* pulling the wagon was powerful and they moved relatively fast. But still the journey took the rest of that day and the better part of the next. Delvin passed the night on the bench, while Jordan and Embra remained concealed in the bed of the wagon, other than a few short trips behind a nearby metal hill to relieve themselves.

They spoke of many things, none of much import, for Embra was still distrustful of Delvin, as was Jordan, though to a much lesser extent.

At one point, though, Embra did ask, "What do you know about the Sun, Delvin?"

"Not much," Delvin answered. "A man can only know what he's seen. But Delvin is old, and he's seen much, including the Sun. Yes, I've seen it, as can anyone. But to see a thing is not necessarily to know its purpose. So what is the Sun? It's a sphere at the tip of an immensely tall Shaft that moves through an enormous wide trench, called the Chasm, which splits the world in half. When the Shaft makes one complete trip around the world, we call that a day. But what is the Sun for? That's something perhaps only God knows now. Man can see, but only God can *know*. Do you wish to see the Sun, young one?"

Embra nodded. He hadn't really told her much more than Jordan had earlier, except for the part about the Chasm. Jordan perked up at that, as if having heard it for the first time.

"If I were young again, I'd want to see the Sun too," Delvin said.

"Do you know anything about a bridge?" she asked him. But he had fallen asleep.

"What do you think?" Jordan asked Embra.

"I think there's something we're missing here," she said. "Why do we make a distinction between 'day' and 'night' when there's no difference between the two other than sleep? We knew it was night by unspoken agreement, so Delvin stopped the wagon to sleep. Why do we sleep at what we call night, instead of just continuing on until we're too tired to continue any longer? Why should so much about our world and our routines be tied to this Sun that circles the world? Why do we know so little about something so important to our lives? I'd never even heard of it until today. And is the Sun really what I'm sensing in the distance? It's directly below our feet now, did you know that?"

"Is it?" Jordan said. "Let's get out, pull up some of the ground, and look at the Sun."

She laughed. "It's not *right* below our feet, dummy. I was exaggerating. It's on the other side of the world from us. You really can't sense it?"

He shook his head.

They were silent for a time, then he asked her, "Have you ever flamed before?"

She shook her head. "No. What did it feel like when you did?"

"Bad, at first, I guess," he said, "because I'd never done it before and wasn't sure what was happening. But looking back on it, I actually think it probably felt good, and I can't wait to do it again. Do you know when that will be?"

"Two weeks," she said. "For most of the flamers down in the Pens, it happens like clockwork every two weeks, once you come of age."

"Two weeks," he mused. Silence, then: "I'm going to start counting down, so I'll know when it's about to happen."

They were silent for a time longer, until Embra's breathing became slow and regular, and Jordan knew she had fallen asleep. But he lay awake long into the night, thinking.

Near the end of night, he shook her awake and said excitedly, "I've figured it out!"

"What?" she asked sleepily.

"The Bridge!" he said. "Delvin said the Shaft moves in a chasm that splits the world. People would need to be able to get to the other side of this chasm, right? A bridge! And this bridge would need to be raised once a day to get out of the Shaft's way, and then lowered once again to let people cross. Suppose there's someone responsible for raising and lowering it?"

Embra had now come fully awake. "A Bridge Keeper!" she said, catching his excitement.

"Exactly!"

"So where is the Bridge from here?" she asked.

He shrugged. "I haven't figured that out. But at the very least, if the Chasm splits the world in half, we can just walk until we hit it, then walk along its edge until we come to the Bridge. It's got to be the bridge we're looking for. No other bridge would make any sense given what we know."

"But suppose there's more than one bridge across the Chasm?"

He fell silent, unable to answer. His excitement drained away.

"I'm sorry," she said. "But you did good. At least you've figured out part of the puzzle. The rest will come, I'm sure."

"I didn't do much," he said. "The answer was right there in front of us. All I did was put the pieces together."

"That was a big step," she assured him.

Delvin awakened soon after. They all ate, relieved themselves, and then started out once more toward Pelis.

Shortly after they had set out, Embra pointed off to the left. "Here it comes," she whispered to Jordan.

"Here what comes?" Jordan asked.

"The circling thing. The Sun?" She moved her finger, apparently tracking the thing. It crossed their path, moving off to the right.

A few minutes later, a blast of wind whipped Embra's long hair, and made Jordan's eyes water, for he had been looking straight in the direction from which it had come.

"What was that?" Embra asked, startled.

"The passing of the Sun," Jordan told her. "It does that every day about this time. My teacher said it's called a bow shock. That one felt stronger than it does at my house. It must mean we're getting closer."

"It's not the Sun itself that causes the wind, but rather the Shaft," Delvin called back to them. "The Sun itself is too high up to stir up such a wind."

Jordan rolled his eyes and mouthed, "Mister Know-it-all."

Embra giggled.

"That confirms it, though," Jordan said. "It is the Sun you're sensing. You said it was passing, and then a few minutes later, the bow shock." He tapped at his lip thoughtfully. "I wonder if we could calculate how far away the Chasm is by how long it takes for the wind to reach us after you sense the Sun crossing our path."

Embra shrugged, not interested in math problems.

Not long after, she pointed off to the right again. "It's stopped," she said. "The Sun has stopped."

"What's that?" Delvin said. "Stopped, you say? The Sun doesn't stop!" He chuckled.

"Keep count," Jordan told her. "Let's time how long it stops. And let's try to keep track of where it stops."

She nodded. "Good idea."

After what they both agreed was about five minutes, Embra reported that the Sun had lurched into motion once again.

"Tomorrow we'll see if it stops for the same length of time," Jordan said, "and in the same place."

Embra nodded.

Several hours later, the wagon rolled into Pelis.

# 10- Pelis

Pelis was first visible as a fuzzy patch of light in the distance which slowly rose above the horizon as they approached. Finally the patch resolved into a thousand individual sources of light coming from a sprawling jumble of patchwork buildings constructed from sections of metal that appeared to have been slapped haphazardly together and then riveted into place. The structures were pressed so close against one another so that it was hard to tell where one ended and the next began. And they were built on top of each other as well, in places climbing three, four, five stories into the black sky.

Looking at the sprawling edifice of steel and iron, Jordan imagined that the surrounding countryside must be pocked with giant holes where the metal had been unbolted and carried here to be used in the construction of Pelis.

Wood had been used in the construction as well: wooden porches, wooden awnings, wooden walkways along the rusted streets, wooden lampposts to which the gaslights were attached. According to Delvin, the wood was harvested by Darkers from trees grown in water farms located in vast subterranean chambers deep in the catacombs.

Smoke roiled up from a multitude of chimneys, and spread out to settle upon the surrounding countryside. The smell of burning wood, cooked meat, hickory, dung, and anything else that might be burned, wafted into the nostrils of the three travelers, so thick and cloying that it made their eyes water and their mouths salivate.

The light from the city turned the perpetual blackness into a dimly twilit world of green, rust red and grey tones.

At the gates of the city, four Darkers stood guard, passively monitoring the flow of traffic into and out of the city. There was a lot of foot traffic, with here and there a few wagons such as Delvin's interspersed among the pedestrians. The other wagons were loaded with foodstuffs, with furniture, with small gears and sprockets and metal plating scavenged from the countryside. A few glowed, like Delvin's loaded with charged coils.

Delvin and his hidden passengers rolled through the gates without hindrance, although one of the Darker guards did help himself to one of Delvin's coils, reaching into the wagon frighteningly close to Embra's face. Fortunately she went unseen.

Once inside the city, Delvin drove into a narrow alley between two tall, rickety buildings, and halted deep in its shadowy depths. They were surrounded by piles of stinking trash: crumbled papers, bits of rotting food, the decomposing bodies of a few rats, here an old leather boot, there the thick shards of a broken jug. The splattered slime of bed pans that had been emptied into the alley coated the ground.

"We can either part ways here," Delvin told them, "or you can hop up front and ride with me to the Darker old folks' home where I intend to peddle my coils, and we can part ways there."

"Here is fine," Embra said quickly. She was eager to be free of his company, as she still did not quite trust him.

Jordan climbed out, wincing as his sandaled foot came down in a slushy mixture of someone's urine and feces. Some of it slopped onto his exposed toes. He retched at the smell, and kicked his foot to fling the stuff off as best he could.

He said to Embra, "Are you sure you want to get off here?"

She peered over the side to see what had so upset Jordan. "I think so," she said uncertainly.

"Why did you stop here of all places anyway?" Jordan asked Delvin in a tone that stopped just short of being demanding. He respected his elders, and didn't feel brave enough to imply that he was berating the old man. But there couldn't have been a more hideous place to disembark.

"Because the building to our right is an inn," Delvin replied. "Best one in the city as far as Delvin is concerned. He won't be staying here, as he'll be heading home just as soon as he finishes his business. But Delvin would recommend it to you, so he stopped. And he thought the darkness of the alley might be a preferable place to emerge from your hiding spot whether you're staying here or accompanying him to his destination."

Embra nodded, surprised by the old man's logic and thoughtfulness. "Thanks. I think we'll get off here."

Jordan helped her down, and she looked no more thrilled to be standing upon the slimy ground than he. Jordan gathered their bags of dirt, Embra their bags of fruits and vegetables.

"I wouldn't carry that dirt around in the open," Delvin advised. "You'll just be inviting trouble. Best put it under the girlie's shirt as if she's pregnant. Present yourselves as a couple at the inn. It'll make people less suspicious of you if they get the impression that you're a young expectant couple who perhaps ran away to be together. Also might throw any Darkers off your trail."

Embra saw the wisdom of this, so she swapped bags with Jordan and stuffed the bags of dirt beneath her shirt, wrapping her hands around her newly bulging stomach to hold them in place.

"Thanks for your help, Delvin," Jordan told the old man, and they shook hands.

"No thanks necessary," Delvin replied. "You paid well for my aid. Now, you sure you didn't pilfer any of my dirt when you took yours out? I wouldn't want to get all the way home and find I did all this for nothing."

"I swear," Jordan said.

Delvin smiled. "Good! I guess old Delvin's dream came true after all, yes?"

Then he cracked the whip upon the beast's hide, and slowly backed the wagon from the alley. As he did so, he called out a final few words to Embra: "Remember, your majesty, there are no accidents. Everything happens for a reason."

And then he was out of the alley and away down the street.

Embra and Jordan crept to the head of the alley and stood looking after him.

"Strange old man. What do you think he meant by that last?" Embra asked.

"I don't know," Jordan said. "But one of the Darkers who showed up at my house yesterday said they were looking for a girl, and he called her a Flame Queen. He was talking about you, I'm sure."

"What!" Embra said. "Why did you not mention that before?"

"I forgot until just now," Jordan replied. "I wasn't exactly in the best frame of mind at the time to make sure I remembered all the details of what I overheard."

"Of course," Embra said. "I'm sorry for my reaction. But what's a Flame Queen? And why would Delvin call me 'your majesty' unless he knew? But how could he know?"

Jordan shrugged. "All good questions to which I have no answer."

"Did you overhear anything else yesterday?"

Jordan thought long and hard. "Something about a Flame King. That's all."

"Do you suppose you're the Flame King?" Embra asked. "Maybe that's why they wanted to take you back to the catacombs."

Jordan shook his head. "I doubt it. If Delvin somehow recognized you as this Flame Queen, he probably would have recognized me too."

"Well," Embra said. "If he thought I was some sort of queen, he certainly wasn't very respectful of me until the very end."

Jordan thought she sounded miffed, and stifled a laugh.

He looked up and down the street, getting the feel of the place. This was his first time in any sort of large assemblage of people. He had only ever been to a small market in the middle of nowhere, near the well, and near his school too. His school had only been a single, isolated building where kids his own age had come in from the surrounding countryside whenever the whim caught them — which seemed to be not often because most of his classes had only a few students — to learn from their Darker teacher, who had never really seemed to know all that much. Just enough more than they did to make her valuable as a teacher.

The street was long and narrow, running the whole length of the city, about half a mile, so that he and Embra could see from one end to the other. The street was barely wide enough for the passage of two wagons at a time, if they were small, each traveling in opposite directions. But of wagons there were few. Pedestrians walked the street, providing obstacles for the few wagons trundling slowly about town. These pedestrians were mostly humans. There were a few Darkers interspersed among the throngs, standing head and shoulders above the crowds. But these latter shielded themselves and hurried along, obviously bothered by the yellow light from the gas lamps that lined the street and poured from the windows.

There were wooden sidewalks along the streets. These were in an advanced state of disrepair, rotting through in numerous spots, and obviously unstable in many others, so that you had to choose your steps carefully. In fact, even as he watched, Jordan observed at least two people trip. The man caught himself, but the lady went sprawling, and the nearby crowd called out for a doctor. The ones who weren't busy laughing, at least.

There were several side streets that branched off this main one. These were just as crowded, as far as Jordan could make out from his current vantage point.

"So what's next?" Jordan asked Embra.

"I propose that we take a room at this inn and then explore the town a bit. Have a good meal. And maybe by tomorrow we'll have figured out where to go, or at least have found a clue."

Jordan nodded. "That's just about what I was thinking."

He pulled Embra back into the alley for a bit of privacy, and then started to reach beneath Embra's shirt.

"Hey!" she said, grabbing his hand. "What do you think you're doing?"

"Getting a handful of dirt," he said, twisting in her grip. "So we can pay for the room. A handful should be more than enough, and we don't want to drag a bag out in front of the innkeeper. That will just invite thieves; and you're supposed to be pregnant anyway, remember?"

"I remember," she said. "I just thought maybe you were going to try to make it more than a ruse." She let go of his hand and smiled a strange smile at him, giving him free access to the bags beneath her shirt.

"Watch your hands," she warned him as he reached beneath and into a bag.

A few minutes later they stepped inside the lobby of the inn: a small room, metal walls, wooden floor, a shabby wooden counter opposite the door, and a rickety flight of steps next to it leading up into shadows.

A tall, skinny clerk with a long nose slouched behind the counter. He perked up when Jordan and Embra entered.

Jordan stepped up to the counter and set the bags of fruits and vegetables onto the floor while he bartered. "We'd like..." he said, and then stopped, looking in a panic at Embra, realizing that he hadn't entirely thought this through. Should they get separate rooms, possibly spoiling their disguise?

But Embra, obviously not concerned, smoothly stepped in for him. "We'd like a room, please."

The clerk looked between them. He looked at Embra's bulging stomach, then displayed a mouthful of crooked teeth that were blackened at the gum line, and winked at Jordan. "One room, sure, sure."

"How much?" Jordan asked.

"Well, that depends on how much you got."

Jordan overturned his hand and dumped the dirt onto the clerk's ledger. "Is that enough?"

The clerk's eyes widened, and he began nodding and smiling effusively. "Sure, that ought to cover a night or two. We'll throw in a meal as well, at the cafe next door. Nothing fancy though, mind you."

Jordan nodded.

The clerk gave them a rusted steel key with the number "6" etched into it. "Up two flights and to the left," he told them. He winked slyly at Jordan again. "Enjoy your stay at the Pelis Palace, Bub."

Embra looked around at the rusted walls and floor, at the filthy curtains and the rickety, rotting stairs. "The Palace, hmph," she said, sniffing disdainfully. Even though this was no worse than any room in the Pens, and indeed in a lot of ways it was better, since she was free now, the clerk's reaction said that they had overpaid, and so by that standard the accommodations weren't up to par.

Room 6 was on the top floor at the end of a dim narrow hallway lit by a single flickering gas lamp halfway between the stairs and the door. The floor was carpeted, but the carpet was old and stained and had blue mold growing in scattered splotches. The walls, made of wood and papered with a pattern of faded blue stripes and red roses, was equally stained. Jordan suspected the roof must leak. The only other door on the floor was standing halfway open and was dark within. A powerful odor of unwashed bodies emanated from it, and something rustled within, sounding like a rodent scurrying among papers.

"Either Delvin has very low standards," Embra commented, "or we don't want to see the other inns in Pelis."

Jordan snickered, and slid the key into the lock of Room 6.

It was a small, dingy room with a lopsided dresser, a rickety wooden chair, and a lumpy bed big enough for two. There was a chamber pot sticking half out from beneath the bed, and a double-paned window barely big enough to dump out the chamber pot through along the wall opposite the door.

Jordan set his bags down in one corner.

"I hope you find the floor comfortable enough," Embra said, sitting down on the edge of the bed. She pulled the bags out from beneath her shirt.

Jordan looked dubiously at the stained carpeting at the foot of the bed. "It will do, I suppose." He squatted down upon it, folding his legs beneath him. "You know," he said. "I wonder where you get your exacting standards from, since you can't have ever known any better living conditions. None of us have,

I expect. Not us, not the people of Pelis, not anyone in the entire world."

"I doubt that," she said. "Somewhere, someone knows better."

"Or somewhen," he said.

She shrugged. "Just because we live in this hellhole of a world doesn't mean we can't know it should be better. The greater the darkness, the stronger the need for light. For us humans, at least."

"Why don't we go out and look around, get a meal," he suggested. "Let's fill our pockets with dirt."

"If we must," she said.

They each scooped out a few handfuls, and jammed the dirt into their pockets. Then, while Jordan hid the two bags of dirt underneath the bed, Embra took one of the two dirty, lumpy pillows from the bed and shoved it beneath her shirt.

"How long do I have to keep up this little ruse?" she asked. "Why did I ever let myself be talked into it? It will get tiresome very quickly."

"We could stop it in the morning and tell anyone who asks that you gave birth overnight and we threw out the baby with the pot water," Jordan suggested.

"That's terrible," Embra said. "You shouldn't say such things." But she giggled anyway.

Soon they were back out on the street. Stepping carefully because of the rot, they wandered up the sidewalk toward the end of town opposite that from which they had entered, peering in the windows of the storefronts they passed, fending off aggressive vendors calling out to them from their tiny kiosks outside the shops.

One window belonged to a clothing shop. Jordan and Embra discussed purchasing a new pair of clothes for each of them, but decided against it, reasoning that new, clean clothes would make them stand out from the crowd, most of whom wore threadbare, filthy clothing. The shop next to that housed an herbalist, for which they had no need.

Next door to the herbalist was a cafe, from which wafted the smell of baking bread and the aroma of roasting meat. They decided to dine there.

But first: between the herbalist and the cafe was a throne-like chair upon which a person could sit to be given a foot-bath by an elderly man kneeling before the chair. Jordan sat, eager to get the gunk he'd gotten on his foot in the alley washed off. The elderly man gave a friendly smile, dunked a pail-ful of water over the offending foot, and scrubbed away. When the man was finished, Jordan reached into his pocket for a pinch of dirt, which he held out to the man.

The elderly man frowned. "What am I supposed to do with a mere thimbleful of dirt?"

Jordan had to agree with the sentiment. There wasn't much one could do with such a paltry amount of soil. You could grow nothing in such a small amount, and from what Jordan had thus far observed through the shop windows and the street vendors, the preferred method of commerce was the exchange of coins, of which Jordan had none. So unless the foot-washer received a steady supply of pinches of dirt so that he could accumulate a substantial amount, Jordan's payment was pretty much worthless.

"Just pass it on to someone else," Jordan suggested.

"Conducting business in dirt is only feasible if the amount exchanged is suitably large," the man said. "I'll accept nothing less than a handful."

Jordan sighed, thinking the man was being unreasonable. But he had no other choice. He paid over a handful. The man thanked Jordan and then closed up shop for the day, and limped away whistling happily.

They went into the cafe and ate meals of some unidentified meat, potatoes and mugs of ale. It was the best meal either of them had ever had.

They had the same sort of interaction with their waiter when they tried to settle their bill. This time they paid over two handfuls of soil, inconvenience once again being the reason cited for the outrageous price.

They had a quick discussion, and Jordan suggested they go back to the inn and bring their soil to a money changer. He had to explain what a money changer was to Embra, and in the end she agreed. So back to the inn, out with the pillow under her shirt and in with the bags of dirt.

Downstairs, they asked the clerk if there was a money changer in Pelis. "Sure," he replied, yawning. "Up the street, second left, shop on the left side of the street. Old Farno will be able to help you."

They followed the clerk's directions and found the money changer in a small shop nestled between a tall apartment building and what was apparently a whorehouse, judging by the scantily-clad women who leaned out from their balconies and whistled and called to the passers-by.

Inside the money-changer's shop, Old Farno himself hunkered behind the safety of a metal barrier, conducting business through a narrow slit. Jordan peered through the slit and saw a fat old man perched on a stool, his immense buttocks resting upon a pillow.

He offered them four gold coins for their bags of soil. Jordan told him he would accept the offer if the old man threw in the pillow. Old Farno grumblingly acceded, pulling the pillow out from beneath his arse. A little square door to the side of the slit then popped open, and the pillow came through. Jordan passed through the bags of dirt, and received four coins in return.

Jordan handed the pillow to Embra, not mentioning what had so recently been resting upon it. "Stuff this under your shirt," he whispered to her. There were no other customers in the shop to overhear. "Keep up the ruse."

She did so.

Jordan then turned back to the slot and insisted that the gold coins were too high a denomination to be of practical use. So Old Farno broke them down into smaller coins, charging them half a gold coin to do so.

Jordan walked away from the transaction grumbling about the audacity of people.

"They're just trying to make the best of the world they live in," Embra said. "I just got to the surface, and I can already feel the darkness eating its way inside me. I hate to think about how I'll feel years from now."

From Old Farno's shop, they walked further down the side street. The whores in the whorehouse, apparently having seen him emerge from the money-changer's shop and figuring that meant he had money to spare, focused their attention upon him. Their explicit promises of ecstasy followed them for a goodly distance, and his blush in his cheeks took a long time to fade.

Three or four shops down the way, they came abreast of an open lot between two buildings. At the lot's center was a small steel structure with an opening through which they could see stairs leading down into darkness. Two Darkers stood sentinel at either side of the opening

"An entrance to the catacombs," Jordan told Embra. "There was one a few miles from my house. It was unguarded, and I sometimes thought about sneaking down for a look around. My schoolmates told me I was crazy, that the Darkers would catch me. I was never brave enough to test their theory."

The two of them strolled casually past, wanting to break into a run out of worry that these Darkers might be on the lookout for someone matching their descriptions. But they realized that running would attract more notice than acting unconcerned. So they pretended they had nothing to worry about, but did avert their faces as much as they possibly could without looking like that's what they were trying to do.

They passed the catacomb entrance without incident, and determined to return to the inn by a different route.

Two shops past the entrance, they happened upon a shop whose colorful sign read, "Krakmo's Tours." A series of posters plastered the front of the shop.

One read, "See Pelis in Style!"

Another read, "Tour the Catacombs! See the Underland of the Darkers!"

"Ooh!" said Jordan.

"Absolutely not!" said Embra.

A third sign read, "Take the trip of a lifetime! See the Chasm! See the Fabled Sun! Visit the Bridge at Bridgeton! Stagecoach Leaving Daily!"

They stared at the third poster for several long moments, passing from shock to delight at their incredible good fortune.

They went inside and were greeted by a smiling man with slicked-back hair dressed in a flamboyantly dapper suit. For half a gold piece, they booked a tour leaving in the morning.

Happy that their next course had been determined, they returned to the inn and passed a restful night.

# 11 - On the Road Again

They arose bright and early the next morning, and took the free breakfast promised them by the clerk at the cafe next door.

At one point as they dined upon burnt eggs and a loaf of bread, Embra stopped chewing and pointed off to the left. "There it goes," she said. She didn't have to specify to what 'it' she was referring.

A few moments later, she said, "It's stopped."

Jordan nodded, and silently began counting as he ate. "Same place?" he asked.

She shrugged. "I think so, but how can I be sure? I can't actually see it or its surroundings, and we've moved since yesterday, so how can I be sure it's stopped at the same spot?"

Jordan said nothing, merely continued eating.

"It's moving again," she soon reported.

"About five minutes, same as yesterday," Jordan said, and she agreed with his calculation.

Shortly thereafter, they left the cafe and proceeded to the end of the street where they were to board the bus.

When they got to the appointed place, they found a large stagecoach with three rows of seats inside the cab, enough to seat six, and two exterior seats behind the cab. It was pulled by two of the same huge muscular beasts that had pulled Delvin's wagon. *Mokks*.

Apparently there were to be only five passengers on the tour, and the other three had already arrived. They were seated within the cab, chatting. Two of them were, at least. Upon the arrival of Embra and Jordan, the three peered out to assess the newcomers.

The driver himself was a tall, thin, dour man wearing a black suit and a stovepipe hat. He held the reins already in his hands, as if he were eager to be off. When Embra and Jordan presented themselves, he ran a quick glance over them, then took their tickets. He briefly examined the tickets to make sure they were in order before punching them with a little device he removed from his breast pocket.

Then his eyes suddenly widened, and he looked once more at Embra, this time with ill-concealed excitement. His hand shook nervously as he handed back their tickets without taking his eyes off Embra. Then he actually smiled at her, which seemed unnatural on his long face, but which conveyed a genuine, honest joy.

He said nothing, but motioned for them to seat themselves in the cab. Embra and Jordan exchanged a look of bafflement, but refrained from discussing what the driver's strange attitude toward her might mean, for fear that the other passengers would overhear.

No sooner had they seated themselves than two Darkers approached the driver. They shielded their strange dual-colored eyes with their bony hands, as if the gaslight was almost brighter than they could tolerate. Which of course it was.

They handed a slip of paper up to the driver, which he examined carefully and then shook his head.

"No, I've seen neither of them," he said in a deep voice.

The Darkers started back toward the cab.

Jordan, thinking quickly, pulled Embra close, wrapped his arms tightly around her and ground his lips against hers. He reached up under her shirt and felt her breasts. Her eyes widened in startlement at first, but she didn't resist.

The Darkers looked into the cab, glanced over the passengers.

"Disgusting animals," one of them commented as he moved around a bit to try to get a look the faces of the young couple. He eventually gave up.

The two Darkers moved on.

Jordan immediately pulled back from Embra, expecting her to slap him. But she obviously knew why he had done what he had, and she merely looked at him with wide, inscrutable eyes. He supposed his eyes might be as wide and troubled as hers, for he had never done such a thing before, had never felt the things he had just felt. Was still feeling, in his imagination. He smiled at her uncertainly. The corner of her mouth quirked up, but had no further reaction.

"You know," one of the passengers said, an older woman with a big nose and beady, judgmental eyes that were narrowed with disapproval. "That's the sort of behavior that got the young lady in her present condition in the first place. Let's have no more of that on this trip, shall we now?"

A second passenger, an old man who might or might not have been her husband, it was too soon to tell, grinned lecherously at them both, clearly of a completely different opinion than the woman.

The third passenger was a youthful man who merely sat staring dreamily out the window, seemingly oblivious to the world.

The driver stuck his head in the cab window. "Sorry, folks," he said. "Those Darkers caught me off guard. I'll do my best to make sure they don't bother you again. I'm Belmont, and I'll be your driver for the incredible journey upon which we are about to embark. If you need anything at all, I am your servant." As he said this last, he looked significantly at Embra, then climbed up to his seat, leaving them wondering precisely what he knew, or thought he knew, about his two young passengers.

Moments later, the driver cracked his whip, and the stagecoach lurched into motion.

The crossing to the Chasm was uneventful until about halfway through. The driver, Belmont, told them it would take about six hours, as the Chasm was thirty miles from Pelis. For three hours the other passengers kept mostly to themselves. The older man and woman chattered occasionally, confirming that they were somehow related, although the nature of the relationship was not made clear. The third passenger, the young man, continued staring vacantly out into the darkness, and remained a mystery.

Embra and Jordan exchanged few words, discovering that all they really had in common was their shared secret, which they could not speak of in the confined space of the cab, for certainly the other passengers would overhear. They could not speak of their respective origins for similar reason. Anyway, they had already delved into those subjects the previous day, so those topics were pretty much tapped out. In fact, there was nothing they could discuss without drawing questions to themselves from the other passengers. And there was nothing to see in the pitch blackness that loomed beyond the narrow sphere of light cast by the four lanterns hanging from the corners of the stagecoach, no external sights to inspire small talk.

So they simply sat and stared out into the darkness, mirroring the similarly silent young man.

And then, three hours into the trip, they were accosted by three Darkers who swooped from the sky, flapping in from the darkness upon their leathery wings and alighting directly in the path of the stagecoach.

They held up their arms, palms out, in silent demand that Belmont stop the stagecoach. He did so. Then they demanded that all passengers disembark for inspection.

"This is highly unusual!" Belmont protested. "I have a strict schedule to adhere to!"

"We insist," said the lead Darker.

Belmont took exception to this. He stepped down from his perch and made as if to open the coach door for the passengers to disembark. But instead, a ball of flame coalesced between his hands, from which three streamers of fiery bluish-white plasma shot out and blasted the three Darkers to ash where they stood.

He turned to the coach, from inside which the passengers were all gaping out at him.

"Does anyone take issue with what has just transpired?" he asked, the ball of flame still spinning and roiling between his hands.

All the passengers shook their heads vigorously from side to side.

"Then let us speak no more of this matter, ever, even after we've parted," Belmont said, letting the flame die out.

He climbed back into his seat, and the stagecoach resumed its journey.

True to his word, Belmont seemed intent upon making sure the Darkers did not bother them.

Embra and Jordan exchanged looks. What did this new development mean for them? But the question necessarily remained unspoken and unresolved for the time being.

The coach was following a road of sorts across the landscape. It was about twenty feet wide, and had been worn smooth by the passage of many feet and wheels over the course of the years. And it was obviously still growing outward from the edges, for Belmont kept the coach trundling along at the extreme edge of the road, so that his wheels could keep their traction on the rough metal ground plates there that were still relatively untouched by traffic. The few times the coach drifted onto the worn surface of the road, the draft beasts began to slip, and the wheels of the coach to spin, as if sliding across ice.

Once, they passed a small group of people trudging along back toward Pelis. No words were exchanged, and each set of travelers watched the other warily. What evil deeds might one do to the other, deeds that could easily be covered by simply tossing any witnesses out into the darkness, where they might lie moldering for ages, undiscovered in the cloaking black?

But the stagecoach passed the people without any incident.

Later on, they met another stagecoach. Belmont waved at the other driver, for it seemed both coaches belonged to the same tour company, and the other coach was a previous group returning to Pelis. Belmont warned the other driver to be on the lookout for the people his own coach had passed earlier.

"Be warned," said the other driver in return, "the Darkers seem especially vigilant at Bridgeton, inspecting all incoming traffic."

"Appreciate the tip," Belmont said, tipping his tall hat.

Embra and Jordan exchanged worried looks, and Jordan shrugged. They had no choice but to press onward, and meet whatever difficulty presented itself.

"Anyway," Jordan said, risking a quick whisper into Embra's ear, "I suspect we might have an ally in the driver, and can hope that he might have a plan."

Embra nodded, and the stagecoach continued on.

They passed no sign of either human or Darker habitation. No isolated houses, no cities or villages. They moved through a wasteland of darkness and metal seemingly more barren than Jordan's own home grounds.

He stared out into the darkness, wondering what sort of monsters lurked at the edge of the light in this part of the world. And if not monsters, what sort of people might be out there, passing their lives unseen in the sea of darkness? How many Darker families lurked, watching the stagecoach pass by?

Somewhere along the way he suddenly became aware that he was holding hands with Embra. Their joined hands rested on his mid-thigh. How long they had been doing so he did not know, as the trip was passing in a fugue of boredom. But her hand was pleasantly warm and comforting, and he squeezed it and smiled at her companionably. She smiled back, became drowsy, and eventually her head began to lull onto his shoulder.

He resumed gazing out the window.

# 12 - The Chasm

About six hours after leaving Pelis, Belmont halted the stagecoach. He stepped down from his perch and opened the cab door.

"Ladies and gentlemen," he said. "We have arrived at the first of our destinations: the Chasm."

He held the door open as first the older lady and then the old man disembarked. The young man came next. Jordan and Embra followed lastly.

As Jordan's foot was just touching the ground, the old man, who had walked ahead of the coach to the edge of the light, was heard to remark, "There's nothing here. Is the first stop a joke? To what end?"

Belmont removed one of the lanterns from the coach and motioned for the others to follow as he led the way to the old man's forward position. As they walked, Jordan noticed that Belmont had strapped to his waist some sort of device with a hand grip and a long muzzle.

"No joke at all, sir," Belmont said to the old man as the rest of the group reached him.

Belmont then held his arms out wide and said, "If you will all please line up parallel to these skinny appendages of mine."

The group did so, he and Embra to Belmont's right, the other three to his left.

"Now, as one, step forward when I say," Belmont said. "And caution is the word. Please remember that part of your tour contract contained the proviso that the company would not be held responsible for any maneuvers at the Chasm that proved to be fatal."

He paused to let that sink in.

Then: "And now: step!"

And they all took one giant step forward.

Pause.

"Step again!" commanded Belmont.

Another step forward, and another pause.

"Kneel, please," Belmont said. "On your bellies, as if you're debasing yourself before the Emperor of the Night himself."

They did so, but not without a few groans and a creaking of bones from the old man. "This is becoming annoying," he said.

Belmont said, "Now stretch your arms past your head and feel the ground ahead of you. And for this part, ladies and gentlemen, I recommend that you close your eyes. It will make things so much more dramatic for you!"

Jordan looked around at the others and watched as one by one they closed their eyes. Lastly he looked at Embra, arms stretched ahead, next to him. She winked at him, then closed her eyes.

He then realized that Belmont was watching him expectantly.

Jordan closed his eyes.

"Now crawl forward, slowly, until your hands encounter an edge," Belmont said. "Then continue crawling, — eyes closed! — until your face is level with that edge."

They all began to crawl as directed. Jordan had to admit that this was entertaining, and the suspense certainly was building. He let slip a giddy giggle in Embra's direction.

"I've got the edge!" shouted the old man.

"My face is there," said the young man, perhaps the first words he had spoken the entire trip.

"Crawl further at your own risk!" shouted Belmont.

Jordan's fingers encountered a sudden right angle in the ground, a downward-bending angle. He gripped the angle and pulled himself forward until his cheek rested on its sharpness.

"Now," Belmont said. "We are all here." Apparently his eyes were open. "On the count of three, open your eyes. One — two — three!"

Jordan opened his eyes.

Belmont was standing, balanced on the very edge of a precipice with obviously practiced skill, holding the lantern aloft. The light illuminated everything within a range of twenty or more feet.

Ahead: blackness, in the sky, on the ground.

The ground behind Jordan came up to his head and then plunged straight downward into black infinity.

He felt a sudden overwhelming vertigo, and instinctively reached out and threw an arm over Embra's shoulders, locking her to the ground.

To his left, on the other side of Belmont, the older woman shrieked and scrambled backward from the edge.

"Ladies and gentlemen," Belmont intoned dramatically, "I give you: the Chasm!"

Jordan stared down along the sheer drop, at the web of interlocking metal ground plates marching down downward until they disappeared into the lightless depths. He was at the top of an immense wall whose base, according to all he had heard, was at the center of the planet.

As Jordan looked downward, he noticed dark openings peppering the cliff face at irregular, widely spaced intervals. The openings of catacomb tunnels, he supposed, emptying out into the gulf.

Next to him, he heard Embra hawking up a healthy amount of spittle. In fact, everyone heard it. They all looked over to her, four faces peering along the line of the wall, watching her.

She let loose

They all watched as the tiny glob of hacked up phlegm dropped into the depths, picking up speed as it plunged away into the darkness.

"Fifteen minutes," said Belmont, and they all looked at him. "Fifteen minutes is the estimated time it will take for that intrepid spitball to strike the Shaft's pivot at the core."

They looked back down with newfound respect for the bit of slobber.

"Godspeed," said the old man, and the older woman, behind him, broke into a fit of cackling laughter.

"If you look straight ahead," Belmont said, "you might barely manage to see the outline of the far side of the Chasm, half a mile distant. But if you do, it will be so faint that it might well be your imagination."

"I see it!" Embra said.

Jordan playfully punched her. "Do not."

"Do so!" she said, shoving him roughly.

"Observe," said Belmont, and he pulled forth the device Jordan had earlier seen dangling from his waist. He clutched it in his hand, pointing the muzzle toward the center of the Chasm, but slightly upward. Pulling a trigger, there was a loud BOOM! and something whistled out into the Chasm. A moment later, another boom, followed by an explosion of light.

Now the other side of the Chasm was definitely visible, with an immense gulf of blackness between. The light lasted only a few seconds, then flickered out.

"Won't that flash draw the Darkers?" Jordan whispered to the driver.

"No," Belmont replied, returning the device to his waist. "They expect it at this time. It would be more likely to attract notice if it didn't show up on schedule."

He winked at Jordan, then said loudly, "Stand as you will, here on the precipice, and contemplate your insignificance next to this vast gulf. And imagine: how much greater is your insignificance compared to the vast gulf of the heavens!"

They stayed at the edge of the Chasm for an hour. Then Belmont called them all back to the coach. "We should arrive in Bridgeton in about an hour," he explained. "Once you're settled into the inn, you'll be able to look into the Chasm to your heart's content. And then tomorrow: the Shaft!"

They climbed inside, and the stagecoach resumed its journey.

Their route now took them alongside the Chasm, following the same well-worn road as before. The Chasm lay about thirty feet off to their left. The passengers, including Embra and Jordan, rode more nervously this time, conscious of the nearness of the drop. One wrong move from the beasts pulling the coach, one unexpected event to startle them, and the coach could be dragged over the edge, plunging to a slow, free-falling doom.

Soon, a smudge of light rose above the invisible horizon before them.

"The lights of Bridgeton," the driver commented through the tiny vent up near his seat.

As they drew near, the smudge resolved into a scattering of lights most likely emanating from street lamps and buildings. Still too distant to make out much detail.

Nearer still, and details became clear: Bridgeton was not much different in appearance from Pelis — a sprawling conglomeration of buildings seemingly slapped together from scavenged metal plating — and roughly the same size. It was built right up against the edge of the Chasm. Indeed, some of the buildings were actually built out over the horrifying drop, perching precariously, supported on a scaffolding of pipes, steel rods and girders. The whole undergirding of these structures bowed downward beneath their weight, the buildings seemingly in danger of spilling down into the black gulf.

The same haze of smoke from numerous chimneys hung upon the countryside.

One major difference from Pelis, though: the combined light from Bridgeton illuminated a massive edifice of metal that jutted out into the gulf from mid-city: A bridge, wide and flat and rusting, with thick undergirding ironwork.

"Ladies and gentlemen," Belmont said. "I give you: the Bridge! Half a mile long, a marvel of engineering and a testament to the skill of the ancient Builders of this our world, spanning the Chasm, the only place in the entire world where one might pass from one side of the Chasm to the other."

"That answers that question," Embra commented to Jordan.

"Which question?" Jordan asked. "We have so many."

"The one about there being more than one bridge," Embra said. "Pay attention."

Belmont pulled on the reins, dragging the coach to a halt.

"We'll stop here for a bit," he said. "It's been a long ride and it may be a while before we wade through the crowded streets and reach the inn. Longer to get checked in. So please take this opportunity to relieve yourselves beyond that small hill." He pointed to a hill off to the right. "One at a time, please."

Climbing down from his perch, he opened the cab door and assisted the other passengers out.

As he helped Jordan, Belmont whispered, "You and the girl please join me near the Chasm. I need to speak with you in private."

Jordan nodded, and as the old man hurried behind the hill, as the older woman and the younger man milled about by the coach to await their turn, Jordan and Embra followed Belmont to the edge of the Chasm.

"I'd like to leave you right here," he said without preamble. "I doubt you will make it past the Darker guards at the city gates. I want to help you all I can, believe me—"

"What do you know about us?" Embra cut in.

"All will be made clear in the morning," Belmont told her. "Let me get these people to Bridgeton and settled in. I'll swap duties with another driver, and then make a few preparations for bringing you into the Bridge Keeper's domain. I'll be back for you in the morning. Please trust me."

"You want us to stay out here overnight?" Jordan asked. "Won't the guards get suspicious if they see you driving into the city after leaving two heat sources out here?"

"Maybe," Belmont said, "If they happen to be paying attention to us all the way out here, which is unlikely. But just in case, right over there..." — He pointed back the way they had come — "...is an area where the ground plating has been removed, exposing the infrastructure. There are hot pipes down there, which will fool any watching guards, if the intervening ground itself doesn't shield your heat from them."

Jordan grinned at Embra. "We've had recent experience with this sort of hiding."

"Good," Belmont said. "You'll find a bit of food down there, left by a friend who has come ahead of us. I'll tell the others in the coach that you've decided to have a romantic interlude here at the edge of the Chasm, and will join us in the city later."

"What friend?" Embra asked.

"Delvin," he replied. "He's a Flame King, just like me."

Embra and Jordan both gasped.

"Make your decision," Belmont said urgently. "The others are starting to wander this way. Stay here and wait on my return, or come in the coach and risk apprehension by the Darkers at the gate. I much prefer the former, of course."

Jordan and Embra exchanged uncertain glances.

"Please!" Belmont pleaded. "Trust me! Decide now."

Jordan hesitated, but Embra jumped in and said, "Very well."

"Mind the morning bow shock," Belmont said. Then he clapped his hands and whirled away from them, heading sprightly back toward the coach, gathering the other three passengers as he went.

The others boarded the coach, and then it just sat there.

It took Jordan and Embra a several moments to realize that Belmont was waiting for them to get under cover, blocking their heat sources from the distant guards. So they darted in the direction Belmont had indicated, and found the section of exposed infrastructure, not ten feet from the Chasm's edge. They climbed down, and a moment later the stagecoach lurched into motion, heading toward the distant lights of Bridgeton.

Once again, he and Embra were alone in the darkness.

# 13 - The Sun Shaft

It was a long wait. The lights of distant Bridgeton provided a very dim illumination, so at least they did not have to wait in pitch blackness.

When they first climbed in, Embra gladly removed the pillow stuffed beneath her shirt.

"Great," Jordan sighed in mock resignation. "One more mouth to feed. What shall we name our child?"

"It's not ours," Embra replied. "This might not be the best time to tell you, but I was unfaithful."

First they had to pass the rest of the day, which they did by eating a meal from the bag of food they found secreted within their refuge. It contained two loaves of bread, a few fruits and vegetables, three hardboiled eggs, and two wineskins, one filled with water, the other with a weak wine.

As they ate, they talked about the surprising revelation about Delvin.

"Do you think he knew more than he let on?" Embra asked.

"Probably," Jordan said.

"Why do you think he didn't tell us what he knew?" Embra asked. "He lied to us. He said he was returning home, but instead, he left us in Pelis and apparently headed to Bridgeton, stopping here to drop off this food. Why leave us? Why not just take us on with him?"

"I have no idea about any of it," Jordan said. "I suppose we'll just have to wait for answers until we can talk with him again."

They chewed in silence for a time, then Jordan said, "Belmont said that he and Delvin were both Flame Kings. So there's more than one. But I must not be one, since neither of them said I was or treated me with any deference, as they have you. They treated you like royalty, but I was nothing to them."

"It doesn't make sense," Embra said. "If they're Flame Kings and you're not, why can I sense *you* but not them, and why can they sense me? You appear special to me, but they don't, yet they say they're Flame Kings, whatever that means, and I seem to appear special to them. You would think that if they're special, I would be able to sense them and not you, but it's exactly opposite."

Jordan shrugged. "Belmont said that all would be made clear in the morning. He's been trustworthy up to this point. I guess we'll have to trust him a bit more."

When they were done eating, there was really nothing to do other than lie around. They discussed going above and looking once more into the Chasm, but decided against it, not wanting to attract the attention of the distant Darker guards.

They also held out hope that Belmont might finish his business early, and return to them that evening. But he didn't.

Eventually Embra pointed beneath their feet, and announced that the Sun was directly under them.

"Long time to wait," Jordan said. Then he yawned and drifted off to sleep.

EMBRA EVENTUALLY SHOOK him awake. "The Sun's approaching," she said.

He sat up, disoriented. "What? You mean I slept the entire night away?"

"And then some," she said. "I was bored out of my mind. I was even starting to consider waking you up and doing some interesting things with you, but you were snoring soundly, I didn't want to disturb you. Too late now, though. Pity for you."

A sudden shrill steam whistle cut through the silence.

They poked their heads above the edge of their hole in the ground. The whistle was coming from Bridgeton to their right.

"Some sort of an alarm, sounds like," Embra said.

After a moment, the whistle faded out.

A steady, rhythmic chugging sounded then: a steam engine. Or more than one, from the intensity of the sound. And probably big, too, several of them working in tandem.

The distant lights of the city provided a very, very slight illumination to their surroundings. The ground stretched before them about ten feet before ending at the black lip of the Chasm.

A sudden loud crack came rolling toward them from Bridgeton, like a seal being broken. They looked over.

The Bridge had begun to rise. It pivoted upward, rotating around gigantic hinges on the lip of the Chasm. In the far mid-distance of the Chasm, light from the city just barely illuminated the middle of the Bridge: it had split in two, one half rotating upward on the Bridgeton side of the Chasm, the other half rotating upward on the opposite side, which was invisible to them, shrouded in darkness.

"How far away is the Sun?" Jordan asked, burning with anticipation and fear.

She pointed to their left. "Not far. It's coming this way incredibly fast." She cocked her head. "No, wait. It's slowing down, slowing down at a tremendous rate."

A roaring sound reached their ears, like the roaring of a distant waterfall. It rapidly grew in intensity. And then a wind suddenly hit them, blowing outward from the Chasm, a blast of air that whipped their hair and shoved them sideways and backward. Jordan, unprepared, almost lost his footing on the pipe on which he stood. Embra, apparently having remembered Belmont's warning to "mind the morning bow shock," had wisely braced herself by wrapping her arms around a vertical girder just beneath the edge of their hiding hole.

And then a massive wooden shaft, like the gargantuan bole of an incomprehensibly tall tree, hurtled into view from their left. It raced past, not ten feet distant, its widest point a mere few feet from the edge of the Chasm, creaking and groaning, visibly losing speed as it raced toward Bridgeton.

Jordan peered up its vertical length, looking for the fabled Sun. But all he could see was the Shaft spearing upward, ever upward, until it faded into the darkness beyond the dim light cast by Bridgeton, faded into the blackness of the sky. Jordan half expected the Shaft to sweep away the few visible stars as it moved across the heavens.

The entire immense Shaft passed their position in mere seconds, the wind blowing outward the entire time. As soon as it had passed, Jordan was suddenly buffeted by a wind blowing inward toward the wake of the Shaft, sucking him toward the Chasm.

This wind was entirely unexpected, and this time he did lose his footing, but managed to catch himself on the edge of their hiding place. He dangled precariously until he managed to get the pipe beneath his feet once again. Embra had no such trouble, as she had never let go of her girder.

Like the earlier wind, this one lasted just a few seconds.

"The Bridge still isn't up all the way!" Embra said in a panicky voice.

Jordan looked to the right. The Shaft had slowed so incredibly swiftly that it now crawled toward Bridgeton. But the Bridge was still angled upward only about eighty degrees.

He bit his lip. It looked like there might be a collision that would knock the Bridge loose.

Eighty-five degrees. The Shaft had slowed even more, but it was going to be a close call.

The Bridge locked into place at ninety degrees just as the leading edge of the Shaft coasted past. Collision narrowly averted.

The shrill whistling alarm gave a last droning shriek before dying out.

Jordan had to remind himself that this must be a daily occurrence, and that whoever was operating the Bridge had it down to a science, so that there had never actually been any danger of a collision at all.

"Imagine the power it takes to raise each half of the Bridge!" Jordan gasped in wonder.

The Shaft slowed to a halt so that the widest point of its circumference, the point closest to this side of the Chasm, aligned perfectly with the center of the raised Bridge. The Bridge had become a quarter-mile-tall building hugging the side of the Shaft.

Embra pointed up along the Shaft, tracing it upward with her finger until she stopped, pointing at a point far past where the Shaft was swallowed by darkness.

"The Sun," she said. "It's up there. I can sense it."

"This is incredible," Jordan said. "What *ever* could this be *for*?"

The god-like scale of it was humbling. Whoever could have built such an impossibly huge thing? Only a god, obviously.

The Shaft did not stay parked long at Bridgeton. Soon it lurched silently into motion and began moving away at a crawl, visibly gaining speed between eye blinks. In seconds it had vanished into the distant dark.

"How long was it there?" Embra asked.

"I have no idea," Jordan said. He had been too awe-struck to remember to start counting.

"Me neither," she sighed.

"But I think we can reasonably assume it was precisely five minutes," he said.

The chug-chug of the engines had not ceased during the Shaft's brief rest. But suddenly the steam whistle began its warning shriek. Seconds later, the Bridge began to rotate back down. Jordan and Embra watched until it had come level again, realigning with its other half to become once again an unbroken whole, a wide avenue half a mile long spanning the Chasm, enabling commerce between the two halves of the world.

As soon as the Bridge was once more whole, the shrieking whistle became silent after a final, fading, droning gasp. Moments later, the rhythmic chugging of the engines gradually slowed and died away. The sound of distant shouts, of laughter, of the gentle susurration of civilization, seemed preternaturally loud in the sudden silence of the engines. Jordan hadn't been aware of the sound before.

After that, it was back to waiting. Their heads stayed up above the edge of the hole for a bit, looking around, waiting on something else to happen. But when nothing did, it was back down inside, to the food left by Delvin.

About an hour later, they heard the clip-clopping of an approaching rider. When they poked their heads up once again, they saw that it was not a rider, but a wagon. Delvin's wagon, in fact, with Delvin driving and Belmont in the passenger's seat.

The wagon pulled up beside the hole and halted.

"Ho!" Delvin called out. "We meet once again, my young friends. Delvin is pleased you made it this far. He is pleased indeed."

"Sorry it took me so long getting back to you," Belmont said on the heels of Delvin's words. "But by the time I checked the other passengers into the inn and swapped schedules with another driver, then ate dinner, got a much-needed night's rest, had breakfast, located Delvin and such...well, here I am."

"Hello, Master Delvin, Master Belmont," Jordan said politely.

Embra wasn't so polite. Without preamble, she unleashed a torrent of remonstrations, followed by all the questions she and Jordan had been pondering the previous night.

Delvin and Belmont raised their arms, fending her off.

"Please, Embra," Belmont said. "I promise your questions will be answered shortly. But for now, let us go into the Bridge to meet with the Bridge Keeper."

"The Bridge Keeper!" Embra shouted. "Yes, let's!"

"Now," Belmont said. "I want us to move as quickly as possible to reduce the odds of being noticed by the Darker sentries. They are indeed looking for you, thoroughly checking any incoming traffic, so it is fortunate you did not proceed into Bridgeton. First, however, I will explain the exact sequence of events that will now transpire."

He pointed to an exact spot at the Chasm's edge, dimly lit by the light from the wagon's lanterns. "Mark it well," he said. "Notice the upturned edge of the deck plate. I shall proceed to that spot and climb over the edge. Watch me closely and do as I do. There is a ladder just below the edge, and we shall climb down it. I will go, and Jordan is to follow once my head is below the edge. Once Jordan is similarly out of sight, Embra shall follow. Finally, Delvin shall disembark and send the wagon on its way back toward Pelis as a decoy to any possible observers. Do you understand?"

Embra and Jordan nodded.

"Of course Delvin understands," Delvin said. "Get on with it, you young windbag."

Belmont dismounted from the wagon and took a lantern from one corner. "We begin," he said, and crossed the ten feet of ground to the edge of the Chasm. He knelt, and carefully backed over the edge of the Chasm and down, adroitly maneuvering the lantern with him as he did so. Quickly, his head descended below the edge.

Taking that as his cue, Jordan clambered from the hole and ran, crouching low and weaving slightly as if dodging unseen eyes or weapons fire, to the edge near the ground plate with the upturned corner. Then he knelt and, heart racing with anxiety, backed over the edge.

Terrified that he would lose his grip and plunge to his distant death, his feet scrabbled around against the sheer face of the cliff until they found a projection. A rung. He let both his feet swing down onto it and then took a step downward. And another, and another, until now his hands were gripping a cast-iron C-shaped rung protruding from the cliff face. His eyes, now level with the ground, stared across to the hole, where Embra's head was just visible above the edge of the hole where they had spent the night. He smiled at her, and she smiled back, and then he climbed down another rung.

The lantern light from above was cut off, to be replaced by Belmont's light from below.

Nothing but metal before his eyes now.

"Don't look down," Belmont said from somewhere below. "Just look straight ahead, and climb down."

He did so. His feet stepped down thirty rungs, and then Belmont, suddenly next to him, said, "Stop. Now just slide to your left along the rungs. You'll find yourself turning a sharp corner."

Jordan did as he was told, turned the corner, and went a short distance further, until the rung ended and he could go no further.

"And now step back and down slightly."

Jordan did so, and found himself stepping onto a solid surface and backing straight into Belmont.

"Good job," Belmont said. "Now you can look around."

He did so. He found himself to be in a recess in the cliff face. No, not just a recess. The mouth of a tunnel, he realized.

A tunnel running parallel to the Chasm, leading in the direction of Bridgeton.

Seconds later Embra appeared at the bottom of the ladder, and Belmont guided her around the corner and into the tunnel mouth as he had Jordan.

She backed away from the edge, deeper into the tunnel, until she stood beside Jordan. She took his hand, and they both stood watching as Belmont now helped Delvin into the tunnel.

Belmont looked around at the trio and smiled. "All present and accounted for!" Picking up the lantern where it had been sitting in the far corner of the tunnel mouth, he squeezed past them and headed deeper into the tunnel, carrying their only source of light away with him.

"Onward, my friends," he called after them.

And they followed, lest they be left behind in darkness.

They proceeded along the tunnel for a long time.

"Are we in the catacombs?" Jordan asked hopefully.

"No," Delvin said. "We are taking the back way into the Bridge Keeper's domain. The secret way. Delvin likes secret ways, he does."

"Are you insane, Delvin?" Embra suddenly asked. Jordan wasn't certain whether she was serious or joking. Her tone was inscrutable.

"Heavens, no," Delvin said. "Or perhaps. I can't say. What do you think? Is Delvin insane? Am I?"

"I know you're a liar," she said bluntly.

"Embra!" Jordan scolded her.

"What?" she said. "I want answers."

"Soon," Belmont said.

They had been walking in the tunnel for about half an hour when they reached a dead end.

Or rather, they reached a hatch. Their path was blocked by a rusted iron hatch in the wall, a hatch with a wheel in the center.

Belmont knocked.

The wheel spun, and then the door swung open.

In it stood a fat old man in a gray robe.

"Jordan, Embra," Belmont said. "I present to you: the Bridge Keeper."

# 14 - The Bridge Keeper

The Bridge Keeper was old and wrinkled, with a small bulbish nose and a big-lipped mouth. His beady little eyes were set deep into his fat, greasy face.

He took Jordan's hand in his thick fingers and shook it. His palm was cold and clammy, and afterward Jordan wiped his hand on his grimy shirt.

The Bridge Keeper lifted Embra's hand and touched her fingers to his lips. "Ah, and our young Flame Queen," he said. "It is a pleasure to meet you."

Embra pulled her hand back and leaned away from him. *This* was the man she was supposed to see? Whatever for? She found him repellent.

He moved aside and ushered everyone into the room beyond the tunnel. It was well-lit, but small, barely large enough for the five of them...

...and for the two mechanical men whom the Bridge Keeper introduced as Tick and Tock. Each was an ambulatory mass of pneumatic tubing, copper wire and spinning flywheels assembled upon a humanoid skeleton of steel rods and brass plating, with a centrally positioned steam engine inside its chest cavity, belching puffs of white vapor as it chugged along.

"My servants," the Bridge Keeper said, smiling at the wonder widening Jordan and Embra's eyes. "Left to us by the ancients. The four that live here with me may be the only four remaining in existence. There is no hope of constructing such devices in this day and age."

"How do their eyes work?" Jordan asked, looking at the single telescope-like contraption situated in each of their heads where human eyes would be.

"I don't know," the Bridge Keeper said. "If I knew how they worked, I would be able to construct one, and as I've just said, there is no hope of constructing more."

Jordan ducked his head, feeling suddenly foolish for having asked.

"Well," said the Bridge Keeper, not taking his eyes off Embra. "Welcome, all, to my abode. You'll find it quite spacious, and my servitors quite capable and ready to do your bidding. Now shall we proceed to the dining room for lunch? I'm sure you're all very hungry, and you, Embra and...what was your name?...Jorga?...must have many questions, questions that I shall attempt to answer as we dine."

He led them along a wide hallway strung at intervals with gas lamps which kept the place bright and free of shadows. There were hatches between each lamp. Some hatches were open, others were closed.

"We are, of course," he said as they walked, "currently in the ground below the Bridge. My domain extends from the edge of the Chasm to just about the middle of Bridgeton. All underground, of course, separate from the catacombs, and all under my control. I am an important personage, for there is only one Bridge Keeper at a time in the world."

They came to an intersection and turned a corner, proceeding along another hallway lined with more hatches.

"And should I fail to raise the Bridge each day," he continued his oration, "the Shaft would collide with it, spelling doom for the world."

"But I saw the Shaft this morning," Jordan said. "It was barely moving by the time it reached Bridgeton. Surely a collision at that speed would not do much damage to the Shaft or the world."

The Bridge Keeper looked annoyed at having been interrupted. "The Shaft extends eight hundred miles above the surface, and has a surface speed of five hundred and twenty four miles per hour. It only slows as it approaches the Bridge because I tell it to. That's part of my job as well; I do more than just raise and lower the Bridge. If I failed to do my job, the Shaft itself would be torn from the Pivot, splitting the world into two halves that would each go spinning off into the heavens in separate directions, and the Sun would come tumbling down to smite the nearby countryside. Or so goes the theory.

"So the Darkers leave me alone to my business, for this is their world now too, and none can do my job but me. And likewise I leave them alone. Until tomorrow, I suppose."

"What is tomorrow?" Jordan asked.

"Tomorrow is a day of portent," the Bridge Keeper responded cryptically. "Tomorrow the world changes."

He stopped beside a hatch with "222" stenciled upon it in bold black ink.

"Josal," the Bridge Keeper said. "This shall be your room as long as you stay. You'll find a comfortable bed and a chest in which to put your things." He looked Jordan up and down disdainfully. "Of which you have none, I see."

They moved on, around another corner, and stopped beside a hatch stenciled with "210."

"Embra, your room," said the Bridge Keeper. "A nice bed, a dresser, and several gifts I took the liberty of requisitioning for you last night when Belmont notified me of your impending arrival."

"Thank you?" Embra said uncertainly.

They continued on to the dining room, which turned out to be a large chamber whose center was occupied by a rectangular wooden table with six chairs. Several dishes had been spread out on the table: roast chicken, a bowl of potatoes, beans, candied skepples, and several salads, as well as five goblets of wine. The intermingling aromas were heavenly.

The Bridge Keeper indicated the spread, which was lavish by anyone's standard.

"I eat like a king," the Bridge Keeper said, "for I am something of a local celebrity, the pride of Bridgeton, a mysterious, reclusive yet beloved figure, someone upon whom they depend to stave off the destruction of the world."

He held out a seat for Embra, then took a seat beside her at the head of the table, and motioned the others to seat themselves where they wished.

"What's so special about you?" Jordan asked, and the Bridge Keeper looked at him sharply.

"I mean," Jordan said quickly, "why is there only one Bridge Keeper?"

"That's just the way it has always been," the Bridge Keeper said. "When I pass on, a new Bridge Keeper will simply be there, ready to step into my role, already knowing the trade."

The food began making the rounds, each person spooning a portion onto their plates, and for a time, all talk ceased as the eating commenced.

When everyone had had their fill and the meal appeared to be winding down, the Bridge Keeper leaned back, steepled his fingers before him, elbows resting on massive belly, and said, "Very few humans in the world know what I am about to tell you." He looked from Jordan to Embra with a somber gaze. "For the Darkers have eradicated all written records of it, and have exterminated anyone merely even suspected of knowing the truth.

"And the truth is that we live on a constructed world, a massive ship designed to sail the heavens in search of God." He paused, watching Embra, letting that sink in. Then he continued. "But it sails no longer. Untold centuries ago, the ship encountered monsters who lived in the darkest depths of space, proceeding from one star to another, devouring each one before swarming to the next, leaving behind a burned out husk, a dead, cold rock floating in the heavens."

"The Darkers," said Embra.

"Yes, the Darkers," confirmed the Bridge Keeper. "Once, the heavens were filled with stars beyond number. But today — look up! Only a few handfuls remain. When in the thousandth year of our holy voyage we sailed into their midst, we creatures of light who blaze with the strength of suns, tiny stars ourselves, they fell upon us, a convenient source of food and energy for them. No longer need they travel from star to star when they had all they needed right here. And we allowed it. To save the stars themselves, we entered into an unholy relationship with the Darkers. We submitted ourselves to them. But not until after a long battle, of course. Not until after they removed the one obstacle holding them at bay."

"What obstacle was that?" Jordan asked, intrigued.

"The Sun!" Delvin cried out in an agonized voice. "They extinguished our blessed Sun!"

"They extinguished the Sun," the Bridge Keeper confirmed. "And then they herded those of our kind who could flame into the catacombs, where they were corralled like cattle, held as a convenient source of food and energy for the Darkers.

"They forbad humans to speak of the past. They reeducated our forbears, wiped out the possibility of any oral history being passed along. And our great libraries were destroyed. There is one such here in my domain, a huge room once filled with the histories of our people, now merely empty shelf upon empty shelf. In this way they reduced us, made us forget who we were and where we were going."

"Today, even now," Belmont interjected, "those of us with knowledge of the past and the true nature of our world are still woefully ignorant in many respects. We have been deprived of the light of knowledge as well as the light of our Sun."

"But what *is* the Sun?" Jordan asked. "I've heard that it's just a sphere at the top of the Shaft. Is it something more than that? What do you mean, it was extinguished?"

"The homeworld from which we launched circles a star far behind us," the Bridge Keeper said. "That star's daily motion was an inextricable part of our biology. And so we mimicked it here. A Sun was built into our worldship. The Flame Kings among us kept its fires burning continuously, sharing the task, discharging themselves into it daily, as the Shaft carried it around our worldship each day. But the Darkers extinguished our Sun, killed all the Flame Kings and the Flame Queen. Or so they thought. It takes a Flame Queen to reignite the Sun, and one has finally come to do so. Only one Queen is born each generation. The previous ones have failed to fulfill their destiny."

"Ieldra," Embra whispered.

"What's that?" Delvin said. "Speak up for these old ears!"

"The last Flame Queen," Embra said, more loudly. "An old woman I knew. She said she was too frightened to answer the call of Destiny."

"And in the end, too old," said Belmont.

"But I'm here," Embra said. "I will do my duty."

"And we shall do ours," said Delvin, and Belmont nodded in emphatic agreement.

"When the Sun returns tomorrow," said Belmont, "the Bridge Keeper shall open the Shaft for you, Embra, and you shall reignite the Sun so that the Flame Kings might feed it."

"Light shall return to the world!" Delvin shouted in righteous passion.

"Light shall blaze forth, and the darkness shall flee!" Belmont shouted.

Their words ignited a blaze of excitement inside her. Imagine a world where light blazed from the sky, lighting up the entire world like a gas lamp lit up a room! She found that she really couldn't imagine it, it was such an alien concept.

The Sun, she said to herself. A light in the sky. A world that isn't darkness, but light!

"Until then," said the Bridge Keeper, "I suggest the Flame Kings retire to their chambers and get a good night's rest to be at peak strength for tomorrow's task."

"A good idea," said Belmont.

"Yes," agreed Delvin, standing. "This old body is definitely not what it once was, and I'm sure keeping the Sun lit will be no easy feat. Such a thing has not been done in centuries and who knows? The Sun may be stubborn, resisting re-ignition."

"Hold on a minute," Embra demanded. "Why didn't you tell us all this when you picked us up a few days ago, Delvin?"

"It was too risky," Delvin said, sitting back down. "All of us traveling together, you and I being what we are. I thought it best to split up at Pelis, and let Destiny take its course. I told you, nothing happens by accident, and if Destiny was determined to have her way, she would lead you the rest of the way here. Also, I thought that if the Darkers happened to capture you, the less you knew, the more lenient they might be upon you. Answers could wait. Until now."

Embra was silent, letting that sink in. Then: "If you were planning on coming here and helping us all along, why did you accept Jordan's payment of all that dirt?"

Delvin shrugged. "What? Delvin doesn't deserve to be rewarded for his help?"

"Give it back," she demanded.

"Delvin doesn't have it anymore," Delvin said.

"Where is it?" she asked.

"Delvin spent it on a night of debauchery in Bridgeton," Delvin said.

Embra looked aghast.

"If this troubles you," he said, "consider that I've also saved a young woman from a life of selling her body for the pleasure of men."

"You *are* insane," she said in disgust. Then in an effort to maintain good relations with him, she said, "I'm sorry. Earlier I called you a liar. But maybe you really were doing what you believed to be best for us all. You may be a pervert, but you're not a liar."

Delvin smiled at her and nodded. "Not deliberately, at any rate."

Embra pursed her lips.

"And what has all this got to do with me?" Jordan asked. "Am I a Flame King too?"

"Of course not," said the Bridge Keeper. He gestured at Embra. "You're merely her twin-soul."

"What's a twin-soul?" she asked.

"It means that of all the souls in the universe, his resonates the most harmoniously with yours." The Bridge Keeper patted her arm. "Don't fret over it. It's just a bunch of metaphysical clap-trap. It's nothing, really."

"I think it's very romantic," she said. She glared at the Bridge Keeper, shook off his overly familiar hand, and smiled at Jordan.

"And what exactly *is* a Flame King?" Jordan asked.

"Just a Flamer who can flame at will and control his fire, rather than once every two weeks like an ordinary Flamer who can't control it," Belmont replied.

"Ordinary like *you*, Jordan," the Bridge Keeper said matter-of-factly. "You might as well be as ordinary as one of the Ashenfolk."

Embra was growing hot from the thinly-veiled insults the Bridge Keeper was continually directing at Jordan.

"If there are no further questions," Delvin said, standing once again, "Delvin believes he shall retire to his room as the Bridge Keeper has suggested."

"I will too," said Belmont. "It has been a long night and day."

Neither Embra nor Jordan objected, and the two Flame Kings departed for the room each had been given.

The Bridge Keeper gestured to two of his steam-powered servants. "Attend them," he commanded. "See to their needs."

The gears of the mechanical men spun faster, whirring loudly. Their internal engines chugged faster, and steam puffed from their legs, hydraulics pumping noisily, as they clopped slowly toward the hatch after Belmont and Delvin.

As the two left, the Bridge Keeper made another mysterious gesture, and the steam whistle of each, mounted in their throats, gave a toot of acknowledgment.

"Let us go into the adjoining room where we may chat in comfort, my young friends," said the Bridge Keeper.

He rose, and led them through an opening and into a cozy little chamber with a fancy, red-cushioned sofa along one wall, a high-backed chair along another, and a low wooden table between the two furnishings, all sitting atop a crimson shag rug. A small chandelier hung from the ceiling, from which came the slight odor of the gas powering it. Otherwise the room was bare, just four rusted metal walls, floor and ceiling. There was another opening in the wall opposite the one through which they had entered. Both could be sealed with a thick steel hatch with a central wheel, like the one through which they had entered the Bridge Keeper's domain.

The Bridge Keeper seated himself on the sofa. "Join me," he said to Embra, patting the cushion next to him. "Sit, please," he said to Jordan, gesturing to the high-backed chair.

With ill-concealed misgivings, each seated themselves as indicated.

A distant whistle sounded, and the Bridge Keeper nodded. "Ah, good," he said.

"Ah, good, what?" asked Embra.

"Fret not," the Bridge Keeper said, patting her arm. "Just a routine functional matter."

There was a clopping of mechanical feet and a hissing of hydraulics, and then two of the steam-powered men appeared, one at each entrance to the room.

The Bridge Keeper motioned to the one standing at the entrance to the dining room. "Tick, enter."

The mechanical man's gears whirred as he clopped into the room. He stopped beside Jordan's chair.

"Embra and I have much to discuss in private," the Bridge Keeper said to Jordan.

Tick, moving with the lightning quickness of a released spring, seized Jordan's arm in a vice-like grip. Jordan yelped, in terror and in pain.

"Seal Joban in his room," the Bridge Keeper commanded.

"You can't do this!" Embra protested. The other mechanical man had chugged into the room to quell any resistance from her, but had not touched her.

"Let me go!" squealed Jordan, struggling in the machine's grip, to no effect. It was just too powerful for mere biological muscle to overcome.

Jordan was dragged protesting from the room.

The remaining mechanical man, Tock, apparently, loomed over Embra.

A third mechanical monstrosity appeared at the opening opposite the dining room, and sealed the hatch. The metal wheel spun, a bolt thunked into place.

"Retreat five feet," the Bridge Keeper ordered Tock, and the steam-powered man did so.

The Bridge Keeper took Embra's hand. "My sweet, I am thoroughly smitten with you. Never have I seen such beauty. Stay here with me."

He stroked her cheek, and she cringed, whimpering.

"Stay here with me," he continued, "and we shall live out our days together in comfort. No one in the world lives better than I. All my nutritional needs are satisfied by those outside, in Bridgeton and the surrounding land. I'm left alone by the Darkers, for no one else can perform my duty. Raise and lower the Bridge each day, slow the Sun, speed it back up, that's all I do. Plenty of free time for other pursuits."

He laid a hand on Embra's thigh. "Join me. Give up this nonsense about saving the world. What shall become of the stars if we drive the Darkers away? They shall devour all light! What good will it be if we are the only light remaining in a darkened cosmos? So shall it be if we drive away the Darkers.

"I cannot allow it. You must stay with me, become my consort. If you refuse, I shall seal you in your room as I did the others and turn you over to the Darkers as well."

He moved closer, his hand creeping up her thigh. "Open yourself to me now as a token of your faith, or your doom is sealed."

"You're a horrible old man," she said. "You won't get away with this. When Belmont and Delvin realize you've trapped them in their rooms, they'll melt the doors to slag and come for you."

The Bridge Keeper waved away her suggestion. "Oh, tosh. I'm not an idiot. I pumped sleeping gas into their rooms. They're unconscious by now, and will remain so until I inform the Darkers."

"Please," she implored. "Don't do this." She closed her eyes and took a deep breath, then said, "I will do as you ask if you release the others and let me relight the Sun."

He shook his head. "I cannot do that. The status quo must be maintained, to keep the Darkers here. Our ancestors knew this. They willingly surrendered to save the remaining stars from the Darkers. We must honor their sacrifice."

His hand began to roam upward from her thigh, and she whimpered.

"I'm afraid you really have no choice in this matter," he told her softly.

"Yes, I do," she said. And burst into flame.

For the first time in her life, she felt something deep within her open, and energy poured forth. She incandesced. For a brief time, she became a star, and it felt glorious. Fire licked the room. The walls melted and ran like candle wax. The furniture burned to ash in an instant.

And the Bridge Keeper's flesh boiled away.

Soon the energy collapsed back into her. The plasma fire withdrew, and she fell to her knees, gasping in ecstasy, naked because her clothing had burned away.

Before her on a floor that was throbbing red but rapidly cooling, the Bridge Keeper's scorched bones lay in a messy pile where they had fallen.

# 15 - What They Learned From the Bones

She got to her feet and surveyed the destruction she had wrought. Ash on the oozing walls. Infrastructure exposed in places. Black streaks radiating from her like spokes from a wheel, marking her as the epicenter of the lightquake.

In the doorway to the kitchen was a smoking pile of melted metal, piping, wires, tubes: the remains of Tock, who had apparently been blown backward and reduced to his components. A pile of mechanical bones, much like the pile of biological bones smoldering at her feet.

She looked down at the bones. The Bridge Keeper had been a detestable man, but she hadn't wanted to kill him. But she had. She was a murderer.

Or was she? She had had no control over her sudden flaming. She had always known she would flame one day; it was inevitable. And she had known her first time was approaching. The Bridge Keeper had simply had the unfortunate luck of being near her when it had happened. And his death proved he was not a Flamer.

No, he was definitely not a Flamer, as a Flamer would have survived her fire. But he had been the Bridge Keeper. And now there was no Bridge Keeper.

There was no Bridge Keeper!

Who would operate the Bridge in the morning? If it was true that only a Bridge Keeper could operate the Bridge, as he had said, then the world was doomed!

She had doomed the world!

She needed help. She couldn't handle this on her own.

Retracing their earlier trek through the hallways, she arrived at the hatch marked "222." She knocked on the door. From the other side came an answering knock.

She tried turning the wheel, but it would not budge.

Examining the exterior of the door, she discovered a simple locking mechanism. She pulled a lever, and a metal pin that had immobilized the wheel retracted. She spun the wheel, swung open the hatch, and threw herself into the arms of Jordan.

When she had collected her emotions, she explained to Jordan what had happened. They returned to the dining room, and passed through into the next room. The room where the Bridge Keeper's bones still smoldered.

Jordan looked around at the destruction. "By the looks of things, I would say that you did indeed flame." He peered at the Bridge Keeper's bones. "He got what he deserved, I suppose."

"No one deserves what happened," Embra said, her voice tight.

He grunted noncommittally, then bent down and picked up the Bridge Keeper's skull. "What do you make of this?"

Embra hesitated a moment, thinking that handling the bones of the dead was a gruesome thing that shouldn't be done.

But the brief misgiving passed, and she took the skull from him.

It seemed a normal skull at first: white, big eye sockets, nose holes, jaw bone with unexpectedly healthy teeth for one as repellent as she thought the Bridge Keeper had been. A normal-sized cranium, which surprised her, for she might have expected the Bridge Keeper to have an abnormally small brain.

But upon closer examination, the skull was etched with a series of six numbers that circled the crown. Lower down was etched a large circle, with what was clearly a representation of the Shaft and the Sun jutting out from the edge. Inside the circle was a map, an intricate network of intersecting lines.

"A map of part of the catacombs!" she exclaimed. What else could it be?

"Why in the world would he have such things etched into his skull?" Jordan asked.

She turned the skull over and over in her hands, examining it. "I don't know," she said. "But I think these are natural formations. I don't think they were somehow carved into his skull later in life. He was born with these markings. Markings that would only be visible if his skin were removed. Which I just did." She took a deep, nervous breath. "We were meant to see these. They must be of vital importance to us. Do you realize how incredible this is?"

"Destiny?" Jordan asked.

"What else could it possibly be?"

Jordan shrugged. "But what are the numbers for? What does the map lead to?"

"I obviously don't know," she said. "But let's go free the others. Maybe they will have some insights."

"Good idea," Jordan said. "But where are they? We never stopped at their rooms, and I never heard any room numbers mentioned."

Numbers?

They exchanged glances, then consulted the six numbers on the skull.

The numbers circling the skull ranged from a single digit to as many as five digits. As far as Embra knew, they could mean any number of things.

Embra shook her head. "I don't think any of these would represent their room numbers. That's too mundane. These are something else. Something of more significance."

"So we'll have to find their rooms on our own," Jordan said. "Depending upon how big this place is, that could take a while."

"Maybe not," Embra said.

She went to the hatch which the mechanical man had earlier closed. When she spun the wheel and pulled the hatch open, she found the man still there, standing at attention.

"The Bridge Keeper said these things would respond to us," she whispered to Jordan. "Let's hope he didn't countermand the order with one of his hand signals."

She addressed herself to the mechanical man. "Can you understand me?"

The machine's steam whistle tooted.

"What does that mean?" Jordan asked.

"Yes?" Embra said. To the mechanical man: "Take us to the rooms of Belmont and Delvin."

The thing did an about-face, and clopped away down the hallway. Embra and Jordan followed, passing through the vapor clouds and the odor of burning oil that hung in the steam-powered man's wake.

"The Bridge Keeper," Embra told Jordan as they walked, "told me that he had gassed Delvin and Belmont. So we'll probably find them unconscious."

The man came abreast of a hatch marked '356,' and pointed to it as he proceeded on to the next hatch, marked '357,' beside which he stationed himself.

Embra consulted the skull. "No such numbers on here," she reported finally. "So the numbers do mean something else."

Jordan released the lock on the wheel, spun it, and pushed it open. Inside, they found Belmont sprawled on the floor where he had apparently collapsed after being gassed, for he was indeed unconscious. But still breathing, as a quick check verified.

They exited the room and went to the next hatch. When they opened it, they found Delvin similarly unconscious upon a large bed.

"Why do you suppose they have so many beds in this place if there's only one Bridge Keeper?" Jordan asked. "Why so many rooms?"

Embra shrugged. "Does it matter right now?"

"Probably not," Jordan replied. "Just making conversation."

"Time is pressing," Embra said, rebuffing him. She could feel the Sun moving tirelessly onward, slowly circling back toward its morning rendezvous with the Bridge. "We need to rouse them."

Embra stepped outside and said to the mechanical man, "Do you have an antidote for the sleeping gas?"

The steam whistle tooted.

"Administer it to Delvin and Belmont," she commanded.

The man clopped into the nearest room and stood over Delvin. A metallic arm was raised, a syringe with a wickedly sharp needle extruded from a finger. The mechanical man bent forward and the needle punctured Delvin's carotid artery, injected him with a yellowish fluid.

Moments passed. Delvin stirred, his eyes fluttered open. He sat up. "What's happened?" he asked, looking at the faces around him. "Why are you in Delvin's room? He fell asleep, and now here you are, ogling him."

They explained the situation to Delvin. When they had finished, he threw his bony old legs over the edge of the bed and stood. "Then we must hurry. There is much to do."

They all went next door, where Belmont received a similar injection, followed by a similar explanation when he had awakened.

"A most interesting turn of events," he said. "The Bridge Keeper's betrayal is unexpected, to say the least. May I see the skull?"

Embra passed the skull to him.

He turned it over in his hands, studying the numbers and the map etched into the bone.

Finally, Belmont said, "It appears to me that this is not a map of the catacombs, but rather of the Bridge Keeper's domain. Look here."

He indicated a line within the circle that began to the left of the representation of the Shaft, and extended inward to connect with a maze of lines nearer the Shaft.

"This lone line off to the side," he said, "could represent the secret entrance through which we entered this area earlier today. Based upon the turns we made in the hallways earlier, I make this to be the path to the dining room, represented by this square here. It is an exact match to our earlier path."

"I wouldn't know," Embra said. "I'm not very good with directions."

"Well I am," Belmont said. "And it is my considered opinion that this represents a map of the Bridge Keeper's domain."

"Assuming for the sake of argument that you're correct," Jordan said, "why would the Bridge Keeper's skull have a map of his own domain? He wouldn't have needed a map, would he? And he wouldn't have been able to consult it anyway, so it would have done him no good."

"But *we* need a map," Embra said. "And now we have one."

"But why do we need one?" Delvin asked.

"Because maybe," Embra said, "just maybe, the Bridge Keeper's domain is of prime importance to us."

"My thoughts exactly," said Belmont. "Note this square here." He pointed to a particular spot on the skull. "It is marked with an X, unlike anything else on the map, indicating that it is a special location within this complex."

"But what is it?" Jordan asked.

Belmont laughed. "It is so wonderfully obvious, my young friend. We know that a bridge is a structure built to span physical obstacles, such as the Chasm. But what other sort of bridge is there?"

Delvin snapped his fingers. "A room from which a ship is commanded!"

"Precisely," Belmont said. "The Bridge Keeper controls the Bridge from here. Our world is a ship, and if you command one function of the ship from here, it makes sense that you would command all functions from here. The X on this map marks the location of the actual command deck of this worldship. And this entire complex, the Bridge Keeper's domain, must have housed the command crew of the ship."

"And we need to know where the bridge is so we can resume the mission of our ancestors," Embra said. "We are planning to get the ship moving again once we reignite the Sun, aren't we?"

They all exchanged glances.

"Honestly, I don't think we had thought that far ahead," said Delvin.

"Well, that's what we're going to do," Embra said. She had never felt so utterly certain about anything in her life. Resuming the voyage was absolutely the right thing to do.

"But first things first," she continued. "The Bridge Keeper is dead. How are we going to raise the Bridge in the morning?"

"We're not," Belmont said. "The new Bridge Keeper is."

They all looked at him, mystified.

He elaborated. "The Bridge Keeper said that when he died, a new Bridge Keeper would be there to take his place. And I believe I have met him. Embra, Jordan, you remember the young man who shared the stagecoach with you?"

"The quiet guy," Jordan said.

"We remember him," Embra said.

"Well, last night," Belmont said. "I had a drink with him in the tavern of the inn, and he spoke to me at great length. He said he had come to Bridgeton because he had felt compelled without knowing why. All his life he had been fascinated with the Bridge. He had learned everything he could about it, which was not much. But he had never been here. A week past, he began having dreams about the Bridge, and a feeling of urgency to see the Bridge in person. So he came. Quite a distance, I might add. From literally half the world away.

"And during his travel here, he felt out of sorts with himself, unable to concentrate. He said he felt like new ideas and new knowledge were seeping into his mind from elsewhere, making him feel disconnected from the world. That's the best he was able to explain the sensation. But last night it ended, and he felt more alive and more himself than he ever had in his life. It seems to me now that perhaps something, some force that governs the universe—"

"You mean God?" Embra asked.

"Destiny?" Jordan put in.

Belmont shrugged. "God. Destiny. Perhaps. Or simply some strange bond that connects us all to one another, or connects each Bridge Keeper to his successor, something in our biology. I don't know. Whatever it is, perhaps it knew that the old Bridge Keeper was about to die, and so prepared the new Bridge Keeper to assume his place."

They were silent for a time as they mulled this over.

Finally, Embra said, "So what do you suggest we do?"

Belmont pulled at his chin. "Well, why don't I go up into the city and fetch the young man in question. His name is Telnon, by the way. He may even be waiting eagerly for us to bring him here. Meanwhile, perhaps the three of you should follow the map to the bridge."

Embra nodded. "Excellent suggestions."

"I've got a better idea," Jordan said.

He stepped from Belmont's room and said to the mechanical man, "Take us to the bridge. Not the Bridge across the Chasm, but the command deck."

They all waited expectantly.

The mechanical man just stood there.

"Did you understand me?" Jordan asked.

The whistle tooted once.

"Then take us to the bridge," Embra repeated.

Again the man just stood there.

"Do you know where the bridge is?" Jordan asked.

One toot.

"Will you take us there?"

Two toots.

"No?" Embra asked.

"Why not?" Jordan asked the man.

But the question was apparently too broad for the mechanical man to respond.

"It makes sense," said Belmont, "that the Bridge Keeper would have ordered them not to lead anyone to the bridge, for reasons of security."

Embra and Jordan slowly nodded.

"I therefore suggest," said Belmont, "that we follow my previous proposal."

With things decided, Belmont departed for Bridgeton.

Meanwhile, Embra, Jordan and Delvin, with the aid of the map on the skull, set off in search of the bridge.

# 16 - The Bridge

Leaving the steam-powered man behind, they passed through a succession of long hallways lined with hatches. They turned corners, they passed through large open areas that weren't really rooms so much as brief stretches where the hallways widened enough that those areas could almost be considered rooms. Their functions weren't clear, but some of them contained several couches and tables. Jordan speculated that they might have been some sort of waiting areas for offices behind the hatches that lines those areas of the hallways. Or perhaps resting areas for people who were traversing the hallways, for the hallways were very extensive, a huge maze, really, and a person walking from one end to the other might easily feel the need for a brief rest during their travels.

One such area, however, contained no couches or tables. And one wall of the area contained no hatches. Instead, an enormous window ran the length of the wall, through which could be seen a series of interlocking gears, some large, some small, some mid-sized. The gears were not currently spinning, but they appeared well-oiled and rust-free. Jordan speculated that the view through the window might be a glimpse of the mechanism that raised and lowered the Bridge.

There was a lone hatch at one end of the long window. Stenciled on the hatch was, "Engineers Only Beyond This Point," which Jordan claimed as evidence that his speculation regarding the gears was correct.

They opened some of the hatches they passed. Not all of them, just a reasonable sampling, to get a better idea of the nature of the bridge complex as they began to call it, which seemed more apt and less wordy than "The Bridge Keeper's domain."

The rooms they sampled were bedrooms. They were offices, consisting of a desk and a few chairs. One room, with numerous long tables and an adjoining kitchen, was obviously some sort of cafeteria.

There was a room with a central table and a huge number of charts hanging upon the walls. If you lifted one chart, there was another hanging behind it, and another hanging behind that one, and so on. Some of the charts were filled with dots, each with a little annotation beside it, such as "Tarl's Star, Five Planets, One habitable." Other charts contained a central sphere, surrounded by smaller circles that were themselves attached to larger circles that enclosed the central circle.

There were numerous public bathrooms. There was some sort of workshop with several tables whose tops were littered with a confused jumble of sprockets, gears, copper wires, beakers, tubing, nails, nuts, bolts, hammers, wrenches, screwdrivers, oil cans, dirty rags. There was a partial skeleton of rods and tubing in one corner that appeared to be a partially assembled mechanical man similar to Tick and Tock and the other two. They had only encountered three such men thus far. Might this be the fourth to which the Bridge Keeper had referred? Or did that fourth one still lurk somewhere within the complex?

There was a room filled with coils like the ones with which Jordan and Embra were familiar. The ones which stored Flamer energy which was then fed to Darkers. Apparently that was not what the coils had been originally designed for. There were hundreds of such coils in the room: in boxes, stacked on shelves, lying on the tops of tables.

They also discovered the library to which the Bridge Keeper had referred. It was an enormous room, perhaps one hundred feet to a side, with row upon row of bookcases. Bookcases lined the walls as well, bookcases that extended all the way to the ceiling, with attached ladders that could be moved along the bookcases, providing access to the uppermost shelves.

All the shelves were empty.

"Tragic," Delvin said. "If all these shelves truly were filled with books, books that were destroyed to ensure that we forgot who we were…Tragic! No, not tragic. A travesty! The historical record! The scientific knowledge of our race, gathered over eons — lost!"

Embra thought the old man might start crying.

"Have you never seen this before?" she asked him.

"Never," he said. "Delvin has never before been within this bridge complex. The Bridge Keeper was fussy about the sanctity of his domain. He only agreed to let Belmont and old Delvin in when he learned that a Flame Queen was finally coming to reignite the Sun. I never suspected that he did not truly share our dream of returning light to the world. I should have suspected that the Darkers would never allow a Bridge

Keeper who did not firmly share their mindset. Old Beezle! Turncoat! Betrayer of the Light! Cursed be your name among all humans!"

They continued their journey through the hallways toward the X marked upon the skull map.

Eventually they turned a final hallway which ran straight as an arrow up to an unusually large hatch.

"Behind that we should find the bridge," Delvin said. "If not, our theory regarding the map is incorrect, and it represents something else."

"It can't be wrong," Embra said. "It's been absolutely right up until this point."

This dead-end hallway had no hatches between the corner and the large hatch at the other end.

Except for one.

Just to the left of the large hatch lay a normal-sized one. Stenciled upon it were the words, "Shaft Access."

Jordan opened the hatch. Beyond they found a small antechamber and another hatch. That second hatch opened upon — blackness. The Chasm. That long drop through dark emptiness to the core of the planet.

"I suspect that when the Shaft returns from its circuit of the world," Delvin said, "we shall find that this opening lines up with a similar opening in the Shaft."

Jordan nodded.

He shut the exterior hatch. They left the antechamber, and he shut the hallway hatch.

They turned their attention to the larger hatch at the end of the hallway. Stenciled upon it was, "Bridge — Command Personnel Only."

Jordan started to turn the wheel, but Delvin held him back.

"Embra," Delvin said. "I believe the honor should be yours."

She shrugged, took hold of the wheel, spun it, then swung the door inward.

The gas lamps were burning even here. What had she expected? Some long-unused, long-forgotten room, untouched since the time before the Darkers had invaded the world?

But no, this was not a room in which the dust of the ages had accumulated due to long disuse. No musty smell like a newly-opened tomb wafted outward as the hatch swung inward.

There was light, and the same cleanliness they had found in the rest of the complex. The mechanical men, or the Bridge Keeper, or perhaps both, had for the most part kept the place up quite well.

The command deck was circular. In the center was a circular console topped with a glass hemisphere. The hemisphere enclosed a three-dimensional wooden model of what could only be a miniature representation of the world: a large sphere bisected by a chasm through which was moving a shaft that projected outward from the center to a smaller sphere atop the shaft.

The shaft was currently moving slowly around the larger sphere, approaching a red dot at the edge of the chasm.

"Remarkable!" said Delvin. "This would appear to mark the current position of the Shaft. The red dot must represent this very bridge complex."

"So the Shaft is about two thirds of the way through its circuit," Jordan said.

Also enclosed within the hemisphere, below the model of the world, was a circular map similar to the ones they had seen in the chart room earlier. Like those charts, this one was marked with annotated dots. Dangling from the model of the world was a copper wire with a small red bead on the end of it. The bed hung a mere eighth of an inch above the chart. They all agreed that it must represent the position of the worldship on the chart below it, which surely must represent the surrounding heavens.

The position was unchanging. The ship was motionless upon the sea of stars.

A horizontal shelf encircled the glass hemisphere. Upon this shelf were numerous dials, switches, mechanical keyboards, gauges, and split flap number displays. A polished brass rail circled the edge of the shelf. A similar brass railing encircling the base of the metal column which supported the console was apparently a foot rest for anyone standing at the console.

A placard atop the hemisphere, white letters on a black background, identified the console as "Astrogation."

Near Astrogation was an imposing chair sitting atop a dais reached by two steps.

"The Captain's chair," Embra said. She stared at it with respect, wonder...and expectation?

There were numerous other consoles lining the circular wall of the room, each an intimidating, confusing collection of switches, dials, mechanical keyboards and readouts. Atop each console was a placard, white text on black background, which apparently identified the function of each console. Next to each placard was a bulb of thick glass enclosing a thin filament of wire that seemed to rise from the console to the center of the bulb, where it curled through several loops before descending back into the console.

Circling around the room, starting to the right of the entrance hatch, was Damage Control, Security, Defense Control, Life Support, Power, Sewage, Intra-ship Communications, Exocommunications, Information Archives, and Bridge/Shaft Control, the last being immediately to the left of the entrance hatch.

Jordan noted that the filaments in the bulb above both Excommunications and Security were glowing white hot, incandescing like tiny stars. He theorized that a lit bulb must indicate an active console. No other bulbs were shining.

Each console also had an imprint shaped like a hand with fingers splayed. He experimented, placing his hand in the imprint of each console. Nothing happened. Delvin tried as well, and achieved the same null result.

When Embra tried, the light bulb above each console where she placed her hand lit up (all consoles except Bridge/ Shaft Control; it appeared the old Bridge Keeper had locked them out), and the console whirred to life with the sound of gears spinning inside the casing, the flaps on the number displays flipping through several numbers before settling upon a single number. Or, in some cases, continuing to flip through numbers, as if displaying some sort of countdown, or constantly changing information. What it all meant was inscrutable and quite mysterious to the three of them, of course.

She put her hand back into each imprint, and the console shut down, the light went off. She thought it best that they leave things as they had found them, until they learned more about the workings of the place. When she was done experimenting, only the lights above Security and Exocommunications were still lit.

Jordan stepped up the dais to the Captain's chair to examine it closer.

"There are a few controls up here as well, on the armrests," he reported.

Embra stepped up to have a look. As soon as her feet touched the top of the dais, the whole thing began to hum, spinning gears and clicks emanating from inside both the chair and the dais.

They both stepped down in alarm. As soon as they were off the dais, the noise ceased.

"What does it mean?" Jordan asked.

"I think we know what it means," Delvin said. "Step up to the chair again, Jordan."

Jordan did so. Nothing happened.

"Now step back down," Delvin said.

Jordan did so.

"Embra, up you go."

She stepped up, and the whole platform whirred to life once more. She stepped down, and the noise ceased.

Delvin laughed heartily. "I believe this means that our ship recognizes Embra as the Captain."

"It can't be," Embra said.

"It can, and is," Delvin said.

Jordan smiled at her. "Good for you, Embra. Congratulations."

"Thanks?" she asked, not so sure that her being captain was a good thing. For her or for the world. The world — the ship? It was hard to get used to the idea that her world was actually some sort of vessel designed to sail among the stars.

In silence, the three of them stood looking around the bridge for long moments, each lost in private thought.

Then Delvin clapped his hands for attention and said, "Well, time is pressing. The Sun moves ever on, and will soon be back here. Perhaps we had best head to the main entrance of this complex and see if Belmont has returned with his new Bridge Keeper."

Although Delvin had entered and exited the complex the previous day, he did not know the layout well enough to find his way to an entrance. So they consulted the skull map and found a hallway that ended in a circle at the perimeter of the map. Assuming that to be the main entrance, they began wending their way through the maze of hallways.

At one point, they came across one of the mechanical men, just standing idly along a wall, and commanded him to lead them to the entrance that the old Bridge Keeper used. From then on, it was easy going, and they arrived at the entrance in quick time.

The entrance turned out to be just another non-descript hatch at the end of a long hallway. The mechanical man stood aside as they spun the wheel.

Beyond the hatch, they found a small antechamber and a second hatch. Opening this second hatch, they found themselves looking out at a large iron garbage dumpster to the right of the hatch. The dumpster was itself pressed close against a wall at the end of a long, dark, narrow alleyway between two tall, poorly constructed buildings. This alleyway was very similar to the one Embra and Jordan had encountered in Pelis: smelly, the ground slick with sewage. Other liquid waste oozed down the walls, and bits of trash littered the entire area, as if no one had thought to bother placing it in the large garbage dumpster.

At the end of the alley, two people leaned against the wall of the alley mouth, silhouetted by the soft yellow light from the gas lamps that lined the street beyond.

The hatch had no wheel on the exterior side, no knobs or other obvious means of opening it from outside. When closed, it would appear merely as another section of rusted metal among all the other sections from which the surrounding buildings were constructed.

"This is the main entrance?" Embra asked. "This entrance seems as secret as the one we used earlier today."

"No, this isn't the main entrance," Delvin said. "If you'd been following along on the map rather than relying on the mechanical man, you probably would have noticed that we didn't arrive at the circle indicated on the skull. The main entrance is quite visible from the outside, and is a prominent landmark in Bridgeton. It's also guarded by several Darkers. I don't think it's been opened in hundreds of years. Maybe it isn't even possible to open it now; it may have rusted shut. There are also numerous side entrances in Bridgeton. The Darkers don't know about all of them. This is one such. The one we entered through, the one a few miles outside Bridgeton, is truly the most secret of them all."

Delvin and Embra stayed at the hatch, holding it open, as they were unsure if they would be able to get back inside if it should shut behind them. Jordan, meanwhile, crept forward to the mouth of the alley, becoming a third silhouette who interacted briefly with the other two silhouettes. Moments later, the three silhouettes walked deeper into the alley, resolving themselves into Belmont, Jordan, and the young man Embra remembered traveled with on the stagecoach.

"Telnon," Belmont introduced the young man.

Brief pleasantries were exchanged, then the five of them retreated back into the bridge complex. The hatch was firmly closed, the lock slid into place.

They retraced their path back to the bridge. Belmont looked around in awe, having never seen it before.

As Belmont explored on his own, the other three stood with Telnon in front of the console marked "Bridge/Shaft Control."

"Amazing," he said. "I feel like I've seen this before. And I have. In my dreams over the past month or so. But it's more than that. I feel like I've stood here before. Like I've operated these switches and dials before."

"Then you know what to do?" Embra asked. "You know how to control the Bridge and the Shaft?"

Telnon hesitated, then nodded. "Yes," he said uncertainly. Then, more confidently: "Yes. Yes, absolutely I do."

Belmont had finished his exploration and joined them. "Do any of these other consoles look familiar to you?" he asked.

Telnon wandered around the bridge, examining everything closely. Upon returning to Bridge/Shaft Control where the others waited expectantly, he said, "No, nothing looks familiar except this." He patted the console before them.

"But you can operate this?" Embra asked again.

"Without a doubt," Telnon replied.

"Then tomorrow, we reignite the Sun and change the world!" she said with great anticipation in her voice. "But tonight, we rest."

And rest they did, after one of the mechanical men served them a fine meal in the dining room.

# 17 - Flames of the Sun

Embra stayed awake most of the night, merely lying in her bed, unable to sleep. She was painfully aware of the approaching Shaft, and was anxious about whether Telnon really would be able to perform his duties as the new Bridge Keeper, duties he had never actually performed, nor even been taught by someone who had.

Where had his knowledge come from?

When she sensed that the Shaft was getting too close for comfort, she ran around pounding on doors, waking everyone up. They all went to the bridge.

Telnon took his station before Bridge/Shaft Control.

As he placed his palm into the hand-shaped imprint on the console surface, Embra held her breath. Would it accept him as Bridge Keeper?

Seconds passed...

...and the light atop the console flickered on. The sound of whirring and ratcheting gears sounded from within.

Embra let out her breath and smiled around at the others. The world was spared the calamitous collision about which the previous Bridge Keeper had warned!

Telnon expertly began flipping switches, consulting readouts, and turning dials in response to numbers which made no sense to anyone but him.

Embra and Jordan went to the Astrogation console at the center of the room and looked at the model in the bubble. The Shaft was noticeably slowing, apparently obeying whatever commands Telnon was entering into his own console.

Delvin and Belmont joined them at Astrogation.

"We need to have a plan ready when the Shaft stops," Belmont said. "We only get five minutes, and must make them count."

"*Do* we only have five minutes?" she asked. She called to Telnon: "Telnon, can you control how long the Shaft is stopped here?"

He didn't answer immediately. Instead, he looked his console over, examining readouts, reading the labels on some of the switches. Finally, he answered, "Yes. Five minutes is the default setting. How long would you like the Shaft to be docked?"

Docked?

She let that pass. Looking at the others, she asked, "How long do you think we'll need?"

"How can we know, as this hasn't been done in hundreds of years?" Delvin said.

"Not too long," Belmont said. "The Darkers are going to know something is wrong when the Sun ignites. Obviously! But the longer it takes us to figure out how to do that — the longer the Shaft is stopped here and we're unsuccessful — the more time they will have to attempt to stop us once they realize the Shaft has been here for an abnormal length. We need to do whatever we're going to do quickly."

"But we can't do that without knowing a whole lot more about the Sun and the Shaft than we do now," Jordan said, "which is not much at all."

Embra nodded. "Then how about this: we stop the Shaft for five minutes, go through the hatch just outside this room, and see what we see. After five minutes, we will surely know more than we know now. If that's not enough time to accomplish our goal, we'll send the Shaft on its way once more, and cogitate upon it for another day in light of whatever new knowledge we've gained."

"And perhaps we'll be more prepared tomorrow," Delvin said. "Excellent, Captain!"

"Captain?" Belmont said.

"Did we not mention that part?" asked Delvin.

"Raising the Bridge now," Telnon suddenly called out.

The others hurried over to his console. Without explaining what it was, he indicated a gauge that was slowly rising from 0 to 100. No explanation was needed, for it was obvious to all of them: when the needle reached 100, the Bridge would be fully in its upright position.

Embra felt the floor beneath her feet begin to vibrate, she supposed due to the working of the steam engines that labored to raise the Bridge. The very air itself thrummed with the effort of the distant machines.

Belmont headed for the room's entrance hatch. "Best we be ready at Shaft Access," he explained. All except Telnon followed him.

They opened the first hatch, passed through into the antechamber beyond, and stood tensely before the second.

"Stand ready!" Telnon called from around the corner, at his station just inside the bridge.

Beyond the second hatch, there came the sudden sound of a great wind outside, almost like the roaring of a hurricane. It must be a powerful wind indeed, Embra thought, to be audible even through the thick walls and hatch. And the inhabitants of Bridgeton had that to deal with every day! Not to mention the buildings of the city, which, she supposed, couldn't be as poorly constructed as those of Pelis had seemed to be, not and be able to withstand such a wind.

The sound of the wind was followed momentarily by a groaning and creaking beyond the hatch, and then a loud CRACK! and a BOOM! that shook the walls. Then: silence, utter and ominous. A sense some massive new weight beyond the hatch.

And directly above her, far above her, Embra sensed the Sun.

"The Shaft has stopped," called Belmont. "I'll let you know when five minutes have passed. You can give me further instructions at that point."

Together, Jordan and Belmont turned the wheel of the hatch, and dragged it open.

Beyond, where yesterday there had been black emptiness when they opened the hatch, now was a huge cylindrical room.

The inside of the Shaft.

Nearly half a mile in diameter. A room so vast it was almost incomprehensible that Men could have built on such a scale. The floor was wood, with growth ring after growth ring, what must be thousands of them, shrinking smaller and smaller toward the distant center, as if the room were the hollowed out interior of some gargantuan tree that had been grown in a garden of the gods.

Embra had seen wood before, wood from trees that were said to have been hydroponically grown in water gardens deep in the catacombs. But those trees were as myths to her, as she had only ever seen the end product: wood. But they certainly could not have been as huge as this botanical wonder.

The walls were strung with lights similar to the glass bulbs above the consoles in the bridge. Neither the bridge lights nor these were the gas lamps with which she was familiar. These operated on some unknown principle that seemed almost like magic. Perhaps the same sort of magic that could imbue a man with the knowledge to operate a console he had never before seen or been trained to use.

Even though there were so many of the bulbs, all around the circumference of the huge chamber, the combined light they put out was still only enough to illuminate the enormous space with a dim light.

The room had no ceiling. Looking up, all she could see were the walls extending up and up, eventually coming together in a vanishing point far above her head. But she knew the Sun was up there somewhere.

To the left of the door was a metal scaffolding that climbed upward all the way to that distant vanishing point. Inside the scaffolding was a metal cage, a framework of beams enclosed by chicken wire. The cage had a door at the front that could be slid aside, apparently so that people could enter the cage. A steel cable descended from the heights of the scaffolding and split into four just above the roof of the cage, each of the four ends attaching to a corner of the cage. Likewise another cable descended from the heights outside the scaffolding and disappeared into an immense box on the floor beside the scaffolding. There were two buttons inside the cage, one above the other. One was labeled "Up," the other "Down."

Embra thought the purpose of the thing was obvious: to carry people up to the Sun.

"There must be more of these at intervals as you rise," Jordan said. "If the Sun really is over eight hundred miles away up there, that means the cable attached to this thing and the box would have to be at least sixteen hundred miles long. That's inconceivable! So the ascent has to be carried out in stages. There's no other way!"

Embra shrugged. The details of it didn't concern her. So long as it worked.

At the center of the room, growth rings rippling out from it like a bullseye, was a coil. A coil for the storing of Flamer energy like the ones with which she and Jordan were familiar. Except this one was huge, massively huge. Hundreds of feet in diameter, it came up out of a hole in the floor at the center of the room, curving round and round upon itself, coil after coil, extending upward, a metal shaft within the Shaft, like a gargantuan stretched-out spring.

As she looked around, she saw no obvious use for the old Bridge Keeper's skull. In the back of her mind, she supposed, she had been holding onto the notion that it might be some sort of a key that would be needed here near the Sun. But apparently not.

All this she took in with a single glance that lasted just a few seconds. Seeing the coil, she instinctively knew what to do. Ever since she had first flamed the previous day, she had felt the power burning within her, a core of white hot fire which some called the Spark, a remnant of the stars from which they had all descended. She could feel it, and knew that she could fill herself with it whenever she wished, similar to taking a breath and drawing in fire instead of air. Fire from some source deep within her, which she could inhale with a different sort of a lung.

And that was what she did at that moment: she self-consciously removed her clothing, handed both the clothing and the skull to a slack-jawed Jordan, and warned the others to back off. Then she drew in a breath of fire, and exhaled it into the world around her. Or at least she would have exhaled it everywhere had this been a normal flaming. But this time, instead of letting it out uncontrolled, she shaped it, she directed the fire ahead of her at the coil. And a column of fire leapt from her hands and licked at the enormous coil.

The flames touched the coil and bent downward, turning at a sharp angle and blasting down into the shaft through the hole in the floor, as if some great wind were sucking it down to the core of the planet.

She let the flame flow through her. Her body grew hot, white hot, and hotter yet as the moments passed, until she felt as if she were being burned alive. She let the plasma fire flow unimpeded, blasting outward and sucking down through the coil. She was a filament, a wire, melting under the flow of more power than she could safely handle. She screamed.

And then her flame died. Exhausted, drained, she collapsed to the floor, naked, sweating profusely, her skin red and raw, the wood floor around her charred.

"Five minutes!" Telnon called into the sudden silence.

"Keep the Shaft here!" she ordered him.

"Acknowledged!" he said.

Ahead of her, the coil glowed red for a few feet above the floor. But her flame was gone, swallowed down through the hole. This coil had not held a charge as a normal coil would have. Not that she could see, at least.

They waited a few moments, during which time she took the opportunity to put her clothes back on.

"What now?" Belmont asked.

She wondered if the people out in Bridgeton were pausing in their early morning business, wondering why the Shaft had not yet moved on at the usual time. She wondered if the Darkers were wondering the same thing, why after hundreds of years the Shaft was suddenly behaving differently. How soon before they began to act rather than wonder?

"I don't know," she said to Belmont.

On the heels of her words, flame suddenly shot from the hole in the floor. With a roaring rush of wind, it raced upward, a column of blazing fire at the center of the turns of the coil, her own fire, perhaps, regurgitated from somewhere down at the bottom of the Shaft, where it touched the core of the planet. Upward the flames raced, an unending stream, upward toward the Sun far above.

And then blazing light shone down upon them. Not fire but light. Intense light, the light of one of the tiny pinpoint stars in the dark sky, magnified a billion-fold.

The last of her flames emerged from the hole and retreated upward. Moments later, the light shining down upon them began to fade.

"Your turn!" she urged Belmont and Delvin. "Feed it! Keep it burning! Be Flame Kings!"

With fierce determination upon their faces, they threw their arms forward and summoned their own flames, which they hurled at the central coil. Unlike her flames, the flames of the men struck the coil and curved along with it, racing upward, round and round, crackling plasma streamers licking along above the flames, until the coils were glowing white hot, pulsing with energy, lines of wavering heat cooking the air and blurring the sight for the onlookers.

Minute after long minute the men raged and they screamed and they poured out the fury of a thousand stars upon the coil, which conducted the flames and the plasma upward to feed the Sun at the top of the Shaft, eight hundred miles above.

Light blazed down upon them in return, and out into the world. Glorious light! The long night was over! For the first time in untold generations, people saw a Sun blazing in the sky, lighting the world, dispelling the darkness. How Embra wished she could be out there to witness it and share the wonder with them!

And then Delvin spent himself. The old man sputtered out and collapsed to the floor, gasping and heaving, his hands glowing red like dying embers. Belmont followed suit a few instants later.

But the light continued. The Sun burned on, feeding off the gargantuan charged coil, which still flamed and sparked with stored energy.

How long it would last they did not yet know. But when the charge began to fade, others would need to be there to feed it, as it was in the old days. Whether Belmont or Delvin would themselves be recharged enough to do the job when the time came was another mystery.

But one thing was certain: they could not let the Sun go out again!

Seconds later an alert klaxon began to sound from the bridge. Of course, neither Embra nor Jordan knew that's what it was. But the blaring sound certainly alarmed them and made them scramble toward the bridge, leaving Belmont and Delvin behind on the floor of the Shaft.

In the bridge, they found Telnon in front of the console marked "Security," one of only two consoles that had been active upon their arrival, for that was where the cacophonous noise was coming from. He was studying the console dispassionately, obviously not familiar with it as he was with his own console.

Acting instinctively, Embra slapped at a large red button on the Security console, and the noise cut off.

Then, the console began speaking to them. A staticky, obviously artificial female voice said, "Front gate under assault."

The Darkers were reacting to the relighting of the Sun.

# 18 - New World Order

Among the dials, switches and levers of the Security console were four small squares of glass with grey underneath. As soon as the voice finished speaking, one of the squares lit up and displayed a bug-eyed, grainy black and white picture of a courtyard in front of double metal doors. Two Darkers were standing before the doors and pounding upon them with their fists. A group of humans was standing in a street beyond the courtyard. A few of them were watching the Darkers, but the rest were staring upward, pointing, awestruck.

"That must be the main entrance Delvin spoke of," Jordan commented. "The Sun really does light up the world!"

"Did you doubt?" Embra asked him.

"No," he said, but she knew he was lying. She too had doubted.

"Deploy countermeasures?" asked the staticky female voice.

"What does that mean?" Embra asked Jordan.

"I think it means, do we want it to stop those Darkers at the entrance?"

"They're not likely to do any damage just pounding on the door," she said. In fact, they seemed to be losing energy as she watched, their fists hitting the doors with less and less force.

The Sun is affecting them, she realized. They're creatures of darkness.

"How do I tell her no?" she asked.

"Just say no?" Jordan speculated.

"No," she said to the console.

There was no acknowledgment that she had been heard or understood. But since the Darkers went on pounding, the countermeasures, whatever they were, must not have been deployed.

"That lack of response could mean any number of things," Jordan said.

"No, it can't," Telnon commented. "It means we don't understand how this console works. We need someone who does."

Embra and Jordan both agreed.

And then the Darkers attacking the doors broke and ran, crouching low as though being harried from above, spreading their wings over their heads, sheltering beneath their shade.

"I almost feel sorry for them," Jordan said.

"I don't," Embra said coldly. But he had been raised by Darkers, whereas she had been imprisoned by them. So she supposed it was natural that he would have a different view of them.

Almost as soon as she had spoken, the voice of the Security console said, "Crew members detected at Side Entrance 3."

The second of the four squares of glass flared to life. It showed the alleyway which she, Jordan and Delvin had been in yesterday. Or perhaps all alleys in Bridgeton looked alike, and this was a different one. Whichever was the case, four people were standing in the alley in front of the closed hatch. With nothing better to do, they were chatting, but what they were discussing was not relayed along with the picture.

"Crew?" Jordan asked. "What does it mean, crew?"

"Perhaps four more people like me," Telnon said. "Maybe I'm not the only one who suddenly just knew how to be a Bridge Keeper and felt an overwhelming urge to come here. Maybe they did too."

"People to man these other consoles!" Embra shouted. "Excellent!" Addressing the console itself, hoping the female voice would hear and respond, she commanded, "Let them in."

But there was no response. The hatch displayed in the glass did not open.

She looked at Jordan. "Do you think you can find your way back to that hatch and let them in?"

He nodded. "I can. And if I can't, I'll have the skull map with me." He lofted the skull.

"Then go," she said. "And hurry, before they get tired of waiting and leave."

He nodded, and ran from the bridge.

Meanwhile, she left the bridge and went back into the Shaft. Belmont was up and around, but Delvin was still lying lethargically on the floor. The coil was still crackling with its charge, but was visibly weaker than when last she had seen it. The light shining down from above was slightly dimmer as well.

"How long do you estimate the charge will last?" she asked Belmont.

"Though of course I have no experience with the matter," he replied, "and indeed who in the entire world presently could, based upon my brief observation? But I would estimate that the coil will need to be recharged approximately once every two hours."

"How many charges do you think you yourself are capable of supplying before you're done in for the day?"

He rubbed his chin. "I'm so exhausted I can barely stand right now. Assuming we have roughly an hour and a half until the coil depletes, and I have that long to recuperate a bit more, I think I could manage one more flaming. So assume two flamings per day for a Flame King in his prime."

He looked at the prostrate form of Delvin. "One per day for the elderly."

She nodded, accepting this. "Then if we were to resume the normal operation of the Sun, letting it stop here only five minutes a day to swap out shifts, we would need half a dozen Flame Kings on duty inside the Shaft around the clock."

Belmont nodded in agreement. "Only after things return to normal, of course," he added. "Normal being as they were before the Darkers invaded. For now, I would recommend keeping the Sun here indefinitely. Hopefully its light will drive the Darkers from the area, and keep them away, giving us a foothold to restoring normality. Send the Sun on its way now, and the darkness will return, and with it, the Darkers, en masse. We would lose what little we have gained thus far, namely control of the bridge complex, and lose any chance of regaining it in the future."

She nodded. "The Sun stays here. But while it's here, it's going to be an easier target for the Darkers than it would be if it were moving at its full speed. It's just a matter of time before they're able to mount a more effective assault than merely pounding their fists on our front door. And meanwhile, we still need a lot more Flame Kings to help us keep the Sun burning. You and Delvin can't possibly do that on your own."

"Yes, the priority would seem to be recruiting more Flame Kings to our cause. If we don't, nothing else we do matters."

"Any suggestions?" she asked.

"There are at least two nearby," he replied. "Below. In a Pen in the catacombs beneath Bridgeton, I assume. I can sense them." He pointed through the floor at a twenty degree angle from the horizontal. "There."

She was silent for several long moments, pondering options.

Then: "We'll go get them," she said. "When Jordan returns, we'll find out where the well closest to your Flame Kings is, and he'll descend into their Pen through the well, recruit them, and return with them that way."

His eyes widened. "Excellent plan. You're going to make a brilliant leader."

She sighed. "Do I have to be? I'm too young. Why can't you be our leader?"

"Because you're the Flame Queen, the only one," he replied. "And the chair in the bridge only recognizes you. Our worldship knows that you are the Captain."

"Destiny again," she grumbled.

"I suppose." He shrugged, then said, "You said when Jordan returns. Where has he gone?"

She explained about the apparent crew members that had shown up at one of the hatches, and that Jordan had gone to fetch them.

Belmont smiled at the news. "You know, I think we just might pull off this rebellion that we have begun."

Leaving Belmont to monitor the state of the coil, she left the Shaft and wandered the halls for the next thirty minutes, lost in thought. She defined problems, she listed options, and chose appropriate solutions from among them. With a new resolve, she wandered back toward the bridge.

On the way, she bumped into Jordan and the four people he had gone to meet at the hatch.

There were two men and two women. One of the men was elderly, like Delvin. The other three looked to be in their early twenties. They were excited to be a part of the new order that was descending upon the world. They had thrilled to the sight of the Sun shining in the sky outside, and they were excited to see the inside of the famous Bridge Keeper's domain.

On the way, Jordan had explained the situation to them, and they were eager to do their part to ensure that the Sun stayed lit and the Darkers were driven away.

They were excited to meet Embra, and some of their enthusiasm infected her. She smiled, and led them the rest of the way toward the bridge. She entered the control room with a feeling of triumph, and introduced them to Telnon.

"We have a crew!" she said.

Each of them approached different stations, making variations of the same comment as they approached their chosen consoles with wide eyes: "It's just like I dreamed it!"

For they had each come into sudden knowledge in the same mysterious manner as Telnon.

They placed their hands into the imprints on their respective consoles. Embra was gratified to see the light above each one light up. They now had five active stations.

One of the women (Sugra, her name was) had approached the Security console, which had already been active when Embra and her group had first come to the bridge. The woman already seemed to know what she was doing, and began consulting readouts and flipping a few switches as though testing her capabilities.

Likewise with the elderly man (who had introduced himself to Embra as Bolos). He stepped over to the Exocommunications console, which had also already been active, and began flipping switches, twisting dials.

The remaining two new arrivals performed similar actions once their own consoles had been activated.

Embra looked around at the active stations: Bridge/Shaft Control, Security, Intraship Communications, Exocommunications, and Sewage.

"Familiarize yourselves with your consoles," she told them. "Get to know one another. We still have a monumental task ahead of us. You know the situation. Think it over for a bit, and then try to give me some new options. Meanwhile, I need to speak with Jordan."

Embra took Jordan aside and explained to him what she had decided about recruiting new Flame Kings.

"Go down into a well?" he said uncertainly.

"Can you do it?" she asked.

He hesitated a moment, then nodded. "I don't really have a choice, do I? None of us do. We've all got our jobs now, and right now, I'm the only one free to do this. I'll leave right away."

The man from Sewage interrupted. His name was Perry. He was a tall, gangly man of about twenty. Pretty good looking, Embra thought. If Jordan and I weren't already destined for each other...

"Excuse me, Embra," Perry said. "I couldn't help overhearing. I'd like to offer my aid Jordan, if he'll have it. Somehow I don't think there's much need for a Sewage officer at the moment."

Embra smiled. "Probably not," she agreed.

"I'd welcome the help," Jordan said, truly grateful. "Let's go check with Belmont and find out the general direction of these two Flame Kings we're going after. And then you can start helping by telling me if there's a well near that location, and finding us a way to get there as quickly as possible."

Perry nodded. "Of course."

"Good luck," Embra called after the two of them as they left the bridge and headed next door to consult with Belmont.

In the next hour, two more people showed up at the side hatch. This time, Embra herself went to invite them in, taking the skull with her just in case she lost her way.

She found two middle-aged men waiting outside in the alley. The bright alley, illuminated by light shining down from above. Embra was excited about that. She took a moment to step outside and enjoy the brightness she and the others had unleashed upon the world. In the light, the alley didn't look nearly as trashy and repulsive as it had in the darkness of the long night from which they had just emerged. The shadowy recesses, it seemed, had added to the filth somehow, made it seem more extensive. The sunlight cleaned up the shadows, and had begun to dry the muck on the metal ground as well.

It was perhaps the most beautiful sight Embra had ever seen. She smiled, and smiled again as she looked up into the sky and had to shield her eyes against the blinding sphere of light shining far above her, at the tip of the Shaft that towered above the city.

But hopefully there would be plenty of time to enjoy the...the daylight, was that what you would call it?...plenty of time to enjoy the daylight in the days to come. Right now, she had to act to make sure there *would* be days to come.

The two men introduced themselves as "Adler" and "Okeefe." They were not overly friendly. In fact, they had a bit of a disreputable look about them, and wouldn't tell her what they had done for a living before that day. But they were eager to get started, and right now she couldn't be too choosy about whom she took aboard her crew.

My crew, she thought in surprise. Already thinking of herself as Captain! She found it difficult to reconcile with the fact that mere days ago she had been living a life of relative ease in her Pen below the ground, utterly ignorant of the profound change that was about to befall both her and her world.

Leery of the shifty appearances of the two men, she made them swear that they would obey her and not cause trouble. They readily agreed.

Accepting their oaths, she led them into the bridge complex and explained the situation and her intentions. The idea of overturning the existing order satisfied them, and they again swore their oath, even though she hadn't asked.

On the way, she encountered one of the mechanical men. She instructed him to accompany her to the bridge, and to remain near her at all times unless she ordered otherwise, just so she could send him to fetch anyone else who showed up at the hatch. She should have thought about doing so before, instead of letting the mechanical men wander off on whatever pre-programmed tasks their steam-powered minds dictated to them.

When they arrived on the bridge, Adler and Okeefe went straight to Damage Control and Life Support respectively, each approaching his console as if being reunited with a long-lost friend. It was a wondrous, eerie thing to watch. All these people, her new crew members, were coming by their knowledge through such a mysterious method, as if they were absorbing it from the aether itself.

She wondered why she herself had not experienced a similar sub-conscious reception of detailed knowledge regarding her own position as Captain. She was still feeling her way forward through the darkness, but the people around her had their paths illuminated as if by magic. They knew their parts, yet she didn't know hers. It wasn't fair!

"Excuse me, Captain," said Sugra, the Security woman, breaking into Embra's thoughts. She had approached unnoticed, along with Tava, from Intraship Communications.

"Embra," said Embra. "Please, call me Embra."

"That wouldn't be proper, Captain," said Sugra.

Embra sighed. "What is it?"

"While you were gone," Sugra said, "Tava and I came up with an idea. It's not pretty, but it might just help you with the Darker problem."

Embra grew excited. "That would be great! Please elaborate."

Sugra and Tava explained their idea. As Embra listened, her stomach grew increasingly queasy. Sugra was right. The idea was not pretty at all. But it might just be the best, and only, option they had at the moment. If such was the cost of securing their future, she would have to pay it.

She took a deep breath, held it for a long, hesitant moment, then, committing herself, said, "Let's do it."

# 19 - Ultimatum

Jordan and Perry rode out from Bridgeton half an hour later. They were mounted upon beasts that looked like close cousins of the one that had pulled Delvin's wagon: black as the night, with sinewy muscles beneath glistening skin, long necks with thick manes of white hair supporting heads with long snouts. But whereas Delvin's beast had been a huge draft animal obviously bred to pull heavy objects, these were a bit smaller, bred to be mounts.

Perry had borrowed them from a local stable master who provided them free of charge as a gesture of gratitude for the lighting of the Sun. And the stable master was not alone in his gratitude. People had lined the streets, gaping up at the Sun in wonder, marveling at the bright blue sky, as Jordan and Perry had ridden through town. The names of those involved had spread quickly through town, as well as their descriptions, and so Jordan and Perry were met with thunderous applause, offers of food, women, anything they desired.

As Bridgeton receded behind them and they galloped through the bright countryside, Jordan was amazed at how different the world looked in the light. It seemed more solid somehow, less ephemeral, like a whole picture rather than a jumble of impressions obtained in brief glimpses, as something appeared briefly in the lantern light before vanishing back into darkness. Like seeing a whole cube instead of a succession of square sides. By daylight, the world was wide and open now, not a not a tiny, claustrophobic bubble of light holding back the immense, oppressive darkness. The monsters lurking in the darkness were nowhere in sight, leaving him to wonder if they had ever really been there at all. Of course they had. But it was obvious now that they had only been there in his imagination.

The rusted metal panels of the ground were grungy and dull in the light. Their uneven metal edges stood out in sharp relief. Puddles of liquid that had long lain on the ground had mostly dried up in the heat of the Sun, leaving behind bright red splotches amid the dry, rusty dust. Mold that had thrived in the darkness was dying off in the light, showing as pale masses growing in the ground joints, brittle masses that crunched dryly as the hooves of their mounts stepped upon them.

They encountered no Darkers along the way. No leathery wings beating across that immense, beautiful blue sky. Jordan figured they must all have taken refuge in the nearest shadowy recess they could find, or fled down into the catacombs. Perhaps some of them had even fled the world altogether, taking shelter from the sudden light in the black depths of space from whence they had come.

An hour outside of town, they came to a circular, raised metal lip around a hole in the ground: a well, much the same as the one near Jordan's house. It had the same setup: buckets on a chain that attached to the teeth of a gear on an axle spanning the opening of the well, the axle being attached to a steam engine that powered the whole system.

Jordan and Perry dismounted and tethered their mounts on one of the rods that supported the axle.

Jordan thought it would be easy to simply grab hold of the chain and ride it down. But Perry had misgivings. Jordan made it easy on him, and decided that the Sewage officer should wait outside the well, in case Jordan encountered problems down below. There was no use in both of them meeting their doom if Darkers had taken over the Pen below in retaliation. And it would be good if there was someone up top to communicate with in case Jordan ran into some other unforeseeable problem.

Perry looked relieved at the option to remain behind, and readily agreed.

Then Jordan climbed the low wall of the well, took a deep breath, and jumped out to the middle, grabbing the chain. It was unexpectedly slick with oil, and he slipped down several feet before his hands were stopped by a bucket. From then on, it was a simple ride down the few hundred feet to the bottom of the well.

Jordan jumped off the chain just before it reached the ground and passed through another system of gears before curving back upward. He found a lone person manning the Well Room: a middle-aged man who identified himself as Relf.

Relf was astonished to see Jordan, but not nearly as astounded as he was when Jordan explained what had happened up above.

"The Sun has been lit, you say?" Relf asked.

Jordan nodded.

"What is the Sun?" Relf asked.

Then Jordan remembered that most of the people in the Pens had never been to the surface. Probably none of them had.

To them, the surface was an alien world. And the Sun was part of that unknown alien world.

Jordan didn't bother with an explanation. Time was pressing. If the revolution occurring up above failed, a description would be useless to the man. And if it succeeded, the man would most likely be seeing both the surface and the Sun for himself quite soon, and in such case a mere description was inadequate and a waste of time.

So instead, Jordan asked where the two Flame Kings were.

The man immediately grew suspicious. "Flame Kings?" he asked. "What's a Flame King?"

It was obvious that the man was feigning ignorance. Jordan himself had not known what a Flame King was, nor had Embra, since that particular bit of knowledge had been so thoroughly suppressed by the Darkers. So Jordan could have forgiven any ignorance on Relf's part.

But Jordan knew when he was being lied to.

"Please," Jordan implored. "The world hasn't got time for games. If you ever want to get out of this Pen, if any of you do, you'll summon your Flame Kings. I have it on good authority that there are two of them down here."

"Why would any of us want to leave our homes?" Relf asked gruffly.

Jordan almost fell to his knees weeping in sudden frustration and hopelessness.

But Relf relented. "Wait here," he said, and left the Well Room.

Jordan looked upward and saw the world above as a bright dot of light against the blackness of the surrounding walls. It looked like a star against the black sky, a view he was used to.

Then he looked around the room, thinking to himself, "So this is what the bottom of the wells look like." All the times he'd been to the well throughout his life to get food for his parents, and he had never really wondered much about what was at the bottom. How thoughtless and foolish he had been! How blind to the world!

Relf returned a few minutes later with two men, both of them in their early twenties.

"I'm Morty," said one. He had blond hair and a lazy eye.

"I'm Carl," said the other. He had black hair and a purple birthmark on his forehead.

"Let's say we were a couple of these Flame Kings you're looking for," Carl said. "What do you want with us, and what's in it for us?"

Jordan felt his frustration welling back up. Why couldn't they just make it easy for him and come along without questions?

"I want you to help other Flame Kings keep the Sun burning," Jordan said. "And what's in it for you is a nice place to stay and a chance to do something good for the world."

Morty rubbed at his jaw, considering.

Just then, a familiar voice sounded out in the tunnel beyond the room, barely audible above the ratcheting of the Well Room's chain and gear system, but still recognizable to him.

"How can she be out there?" he asked, astonished.

"She who?" said Relf.

He hurried out into the tunnel. The voice seemed to be issuing from the air itself. It was staticky, and sounded muffled and tinny, as if she were speaking from inside a tin can. But it was recognizably her. People all up and down the tunnel had stopped to listen.

"...and that time has come," the voice was saying. "My name is Embra, and I guess I'm the captain of...never mind, that will take too explanation. My name is Embra, and I have a message for the Emperor of the Night. You and your people need to leave, or I'm going to flood the catacombs with poison gas and kill you all. And if that doesn't work, I have a few other means at my disposal. I'm sure you know by now that I've restarted the Sun. So you'll probably believe me when I tell you that I have control over the workings of our world. This isn't an empty threat. I don't want to kill any of you. But you've overstayed your welcome, so this is the way it has to be. You and your Darkers have three days to completely clear out from this world. There will be no further warnings. If you're not gone by then, you're dead. If you make any moves against us, anywhere, you're dead. This is non-negotiable, there will be no discussion, and the countdown starts right now. This is Captain Embra, out."

The people in the tunnels who had been listening looked at one another, their blank faces slowly giving way to panic. Jordan knew what they must be thinking: they were in the catacombs along with the Darkers, and were going to get caught in the crossfire! Or they *would* be thinking that as soon as they came to terms with the unexpected news of how radically the world had just changed.

Jordan looked at Morty and Carl. "Time to stop being coy. If you two are the Flame Kings I came for, we need to leave right now, before full-blown panic breaks out down here."

He himself wasn't experiencing panic. He was experiencing a profound sense of horror. He didn't like the Darkers, but he didn't think their transgressions warranted genocide. But deep down, he knew Embra was right. There was no other way. Hopefully the Darkers wouldn't force her to follow through on her threat. And he had no doubt that she *could* follow it through; the new crew that had arrived must have provided her with the option.

Without waiting for a response from Morty and Carl, hoping his action would spur them into following him, he ducked back into the Well Room and grabbed hold of the chain. It yanked him upward, and he hung on for dear life as he was dragged toward the distant opening to the surface.

Glancing downward, he was gratified to see the two men run into the room, grab the chain, and let themselves be dragged up after him. To his surprise, Relf came too. Jordan was fine with that. The man might not be a Flame King or know anything about operating a console in the bridge, but at this point, having an extra body around to help out would be a tremendous boon.

As he neared the surface, he momentarily considered his parents. Considered running off and seeing them one last time before they left. But if Embra had been right about them, did he really want to know? He preferred to remember them as he hoped they had been: loving and kind for raising him. So he decided against it. Besides, by his actions, he had already committed himself to Embra and this fledgling revolution. He couldn't abandon it now, not even long enough to visit his adoptive parents. Time was crucial right now.

Soon he arrived back at the surface. He and Perry assisted the other three from the well. They spared a few minutes for Carl, Morty and Relf to get over their initial wonder at being on the surface. After all, with the Sun now shining, it was a more radical transition than even Embra had had to make.

Then they mounted, Jordan and Relf on one beast, Perry, Carl and Morty on the other, and headed back toward Bridgeton.

This time the beasts were noticeably straining under the added weight, and so Jordan let them take it slower. He worried that the beasts might not even have the stamina to make it all the way back.

As they rode, Jordan noticed black spots in the distance, rising from the ground and drifting upward into the blue sky like ash on the breeze. It took him a moment to realize what he was seeing: the Darkers had begun to leave. It was an eerie sight. Once, very close by, two Darkers came from an opening in the ground which he hadn't even noticed, an entrance to the catacombs apparently, and leapt into the sky, their great leathery wings carrying them up toward their ancient home. They were noticeably in pain, quivering and grimacing, and Jordan felt sympathy for them. Fleeing through the light must be a tremendous agony for their kind. He wondered why they didn't go through the catacombs to other exits beyond the curve of the horizon and the reach of the light, and leave that way. Were they really so eager to depart that they didn't want to take the time to go that far out of their way?

Jordan shrugged. The Darker psychology, it seemed, was a mystery to him. Perhaps Embra had been right about his parents, and he had misread them his whole life.

No! He refused to believe that.

As they were approaching the city, the Sun's light began to fade.

"We must hurry!" he said, and, risking the expiration of the mounts, he spurred them onward.

But the beasts survived, as did the light, until they made it to Bridgeton. They dismounted outside the alley in which the side entrance lay. Jordan handed the reigns of both beasts over to Relf, and instructed him on how to reach the stable and return them to their owner.

As Relf was leading the beasts away, they went into the alley, and Jordan banged on the hatch. It was opened by one of the mechanical men, who had been stationed by the hatch to await Jordan's return.

Quickly they ran through the hallways to the Shaft Access hatch. Inside, they found Delvin still too weak to flame. The charge on the coil was fast fading, as Belmont had already flamed twice and could no longer manage another.

Thus it was time for one of the newly-arrived Flame Kings to prove himself. Morty volunteered. After a brief instruction from Belmont, Morty exploded into a bright star, and directed his flame into the coil. Minute after minute he emptied himself into it, and the coil pulsed with increasing strength. The dim sunlight returned brighter than ever.

Finally Morty reached his limit, and collapsed to the floor, expended, gasping, and laughing with the joy of having fed the Sun.

# 20 - Valdrake and the Emperor

In the Throne Room, the Emperor of the Night sat upon his giant throne after Embra had delivered her ultimatum. His brow was troubled, and he was silent.

Valdrake, standing before the throne, broke into the Emperor's thoughts. "Despite what she says, it's an empty threat," he said. "She will never see it through because we have her people hostage in the Pens. I shall send my legions into the Pens. If she sends her gases, we shall slaughter her people."

He moved as if to leave and carry out his plan.

"Halt," the Emperor said.

Valdrake turned back and prostrated himself to receive the words of the Emperor.

"This is their world, not ours," said the Emperor. "We are invaders occupying their land. Too long has it been so, and now they are rebelling. They are desperate. She will do as she says, no matter the cost to her people. We can leave and be what we once were: devourers of the stars! There is glory in that. We have grown too comfortable here, too complacent. We have become weak. We fought long and hard for this world, and I foresee another similar battle if we stay, for they are backed into a corner. We can leave and live. We can return to the glory of what we once were. Or we can stay and slaughter millions and fight to retain the very world that makes us weak and complacent. No, Valdrake, we will leave, and let them have their pitiful little world back."

But Valdrake drew himself up and said, "*We* are not invaders, our ancestors were. We are now inhabitants of this world. If we have indeed become weak and complacent, then how can we leave? We have forgotten how to survive in the dark between the stars. Our people will suffer greatly if we leave our home. Many will die."

The Emperor, shrewd and experienced, saw that Valdrake would spread the defiance in his heart and ignite the people into rebellion.

So he reached down and ripped Valdrake to shreds.

Then he turned to Valdrake's lieutenant. "Send out word that our people are to begin leaving at once."

The lieutenant looked at the steaming mass of torn flesh, bone and blood that had once been Valdrake, and nodded. "Your will be done, Great One." He saluted and left.

Soon, the Emperor would address his people, reignite the fire to slay the heavens in their hearts. Soon, the old lusts would return, and once more their hunger would devour the stars.

Glory was theirs for the taking.

And so the great emigration began. By the time Embra's deadline rolled around, nearly every Darker had left the world.

# 21 - The Meaning of the Numbers

After Embra had delivered her ultimatum and the Darkers had begun to leave, Bolos, the Exocommunications officer, had called for her attention.

She stepped over to his console. "Yes?" she asked him.

"I think you should hear this, Embra," the elderly man said.

Unlike Sugra, he did not feel bound to call her Captain. She didn't like Sugra's insistence upon formality, but she also wasn't sure she liked Bolos's uninvited lack of it. She decided it was just one of those things she would have to work out in the days ahead.

He turned a knob, and a voice issued from a grille on his console. A deep, slow voice, underlain by a constant hiss of static. "I sense your flame," it said. "Long have you been silent, and lost to my sight have you been. But now I feel your bright burning, and I come. I come. My consciousness is the light behind the stars, I am the background radiation. I am God. Press on, resume your journey toward my incarnated form, and we shall meet in years to come."

Excitement filled Embra. "It's the voice of God!" Thoughts of what they would do when the Darkers left had been swirling in her mind. Foremost was the idea that they should resume the original mission and seek out God.

As she listened to the voice of God, she had an epiphany regarding the Bridge Keeper's skull.

The voice of God was still speaking, but now He was merely repeating his words.

"How do I talk to Him?" Embra asked, her eyes roving the Exocommunications console.

"You can't," Bolos replied. "I've tried, but get no response."

"Come to me," the voice said a final time, and then cut off.

"Get it back!" she barked.

Bolos fiddled with his console, spinning knobs, flipping switches. "I can't," he reported at last. "It's gone."

"Continue monitoring for it," she ordered him.

He nodded. "Of course, Embra."

During Jordan's mission down the well, two more crewmen had arrived at the hatch and been shown inside. One of them, Naybor, had proved to be the Astrogation officer. He had taken up his position before the console at the center of the bridge. He had explained to Embra that the Sun also functioned as the worldship's engine: it could be moved to any position around the world, locked there, and re-purposed to provide thrust that would propel the ship through space.

She left Bolos's station and stepped over to Astrogation. She briefly studied the console. Then she said to Naybor, "Tell me again how you set a course."

He directed her attention to a keyboard below a split flap display. "It takes three numbers," he explained. "Key the first, press this button marked 'Enter.' Key the second, press Enter again. Key the third, press Enter, then Engage."

"That confirms it then," she said, excited by her epiphany.

She went next door to Shaft Access and talked briefly with the Flame Kings on duty. Then she had a long conference with Belmont and Jordan, explaining the brief contact with God and what she intended to do: move the Sun, and resume the mission of their ancestors. Belmont and Jordan voiced their concerns, which were few. After all, they said, she was the captain, and the ship really should remove itself from the area to prevent the Darkers from regrouping and mounting a counterattack.

So preparations were made to keep the Sun operational away from the bridge and Bridgeton. Then, after the deadline of her ultimatum had passed, the world had to be searched to make sure no Darkers remained, which took a week, whereupon the worldship was declared free of occupation.

The following day, she entered the bridge with the Bridge Keeper's skull in hand and stepped over to Astrogation.

"Do you mind if I set a course?" she asked Naybor. "Or would you rather do it?"

"I'm comfortable with you doing it, ma'am," he told her, and moved aside to allow her access.

Embra looked at the skull, and keyed in the first three of the six numbers circling its crown. As each number was entered, the flaps of one display in a group of three flipped over until each displayed one of the numbers entered. Finally three numbers were entered, and she pressed 'Engage.'

The Shaft on the wooden model enclosed within the glass hemisphere of the console began to move. A corresponding muffled creak sounded through the walls as the actual Shaft began to move. Over the next several hours, the model Shaft rotated a quarter of the way around the model, and then stopped.

She waited a brief time and then asked Bolos, "Are we moving? I feel nothing."

He consulted his console. "We are indeed moving. You just can't notice it. Our velocity will increase slowly over the next several months until we reach cruising speed."

She nodded. "Good."

"And where are we going, ma'am?" he asked. "Or is that a secret?"

"It's no secret," she told him. And then she spoke up so the rest of the bridge crew could hear. "We are resuming the original mission, the one our ancestors began so long ago when they set out from our homeworld. I have set course for a rendezvous with God."

Later that day she addressed the entire planet, with the aid of Tava, the Intraship Communications Officer. Embra informed her people of the mission, and received rousing endorsements from the World Council representatives they had elected.

And the years passed, and the ship moved across the heavens.

# 22 - The Long Voyage

The years passed as the worldship sailed through the heavens toward its rendezvous with God and the fulfillment of its original mission. Once the ship reached cruising speed, the Shaft was again set moving, and the light of the Sun was carried around the world each day, shining down up the people. The world was gradually refurbished, her metal surface burnished of rust until it gleamed proudly in the sunlight. The people prospered, and the long night of the Darker occupation became nothing more than a bad memory. Many of the mysterious technologies that drove the world were rediscovered. The arts blossomed; books stolen from the ancient humans of the worldship were discovered here and there throughout the old territory of the Darkers, and the libraries of the world, decimated by the Darkers, began to fill once more. One such book that caught Embra's attention was *The Book of Light* by Ba'rath'ma'oor, a historical-religious treatise with which she became preoccupied.

She gave many orders and became a wise, respected leader, growing in confidence and power.

One such order was that a census be taken. They needed to know the precise number of people who inhabited the world.

So enumerators were sent out, all across the face of the world and deep into the darkest corners of the catacombs, and all people were counted. The results were tabulated.

They were five million strong. Three million were Ashenfolk, two million were Flamers. Of the latter, fifty thousand were Flame Kings and one was a Flame Queen.

One hundred Flame Kings were moved into the bridge complex, where they worked the Sun in shifts. Twenty thousand took up residence in the catacombs around Bridgeton, to keep them near at hand in case need for them arose. The rest were scattered around the world, to ensure that their kind would survive if catastrophe should befall any one place.

And there *were* catastrophes. Rocks from the heavens collided with their world. There were several epidemics of one sickness or another. There were skirmishes with Darker gangs who occasionally swooped in from the stars and hauled numbers of Embra's people off into the darkness.

Thankfully these catastrophes were few and far between, and during the tenth year of the resumption of their voyage, the year they encountered God, they were still nearly four million eight hundred thousand strong: a respectable, healthy number.

Years before the encounter, Jordan was exploring the catacombs, which was his favorite pastime. There were so many uncounted miles of them honeycombing the planet, and too few people to fill them all. So vast sections remained unexplored, and were just as they had been left by the Darkers. There were even sections where not even the Darkers had lived, sections which had not been seen by any living being since long before the arrival of the Darkers. Jordan loved the mystery of such places, the sense of age and abandonment.

It was in one of these unexplored tunnels that Jordan came across an old Darker who had not left with the others. He had become a hermit, living and slinking through the darkest, deepest places of the world, drawing sustenance from the pilot light that burned at the core of the world, the light which Embra had ignited when they had first entered the Shaft years before, the light which burned still, sustaining the minimum necessary charge for the massive coil housed inside the Shaft.

The first time Jordan stumbled across the reclusive Darker in a deep, long-abandoned tunnel, they were both greatly frightened. Each thought he would be killed outright by the other. But neither was of such a mind. Jordan didn't think it would matter if a Darker or two were still left in the world, and the Darker was too old to be much of a threat to Jordan. In fact, the old Darker, whose name was Jolak, was desperate for the company that Jordan could provide.

So they became friends. Or as close to friends as their differences would allow.

When Jordan informed Jolak that the worldship was on its way to a rendezvous with God, the old Darker grew agitated.

"No," Jolak said. "You must turn aside. You will not find God. You will find a monstrosity a hundred times hungrier for your energy than a Darker. An immense, powerful creature that has devoured all the stars in its quarter of the universe, and is moving slowly this way. Look up into the sky, in the direction of your travel, and you will see a black void containing not even a single star. That is the creature's doing, its ever-expanding territory, and you are heading right for it. We Darkers merely fed off you, but at least we left you your lives. In our own way, we were protecting you. But no longer. This creature will eat you whole. In a single day, it will extinguish you from the universe."

"How do you know this?" Jordan asked.

"Because my kind are its children!" the Darker said. "Once, we lived in its corner of the universe, subsisting on whatever star crumbs it saw fit to toss us. We were starving. We could not compete with it, and so we fled outward, leaping ahead of it to where the stars were abundant. And like our God, we too devoured the stars, until we found you. And now God will find you, and it will be the end of your kind. You must turn aside if you are to survive."

Jordan, alarmed by this revelation, brought it to Embra. But her faith in their mission could not be shaken; she was now fanatical about finding God and completing the voyage their ancestors had begun. She said Jolak was deceiving Jordan, and had the old Darker killed.

Thereafter, things were tense between Embra and Jordan, and they spoke only of mundane matters, for he was her twin-soul, and did not want her to shut him completely away. But every time he looked into the night sky and saw the great star void of which Jolak had spoken, fear for the future weighed heavily upon his heart.

And then, in the tenth year, they encountered God.

# 23 - Encounter

It was the middle of the night. Embra was in her quarters, deep in sleep, when the intercom roused her.

"Captain!" Bolos's voice. Years ago, she had finally insisted that he begin calling her Captain. "Captain to the bridge at once!"

"What is it?" she said groggily, on the verge of just ignoring him, rolling over and going back to sleep.

"We've reestablished contact with God!"

She came instantly awake. "I'm on my way!"

She got out of bed and threw on her clothes. As she was rushing out the door, she was vaguely aware of Jordan stirring in the bed behind her, probably preparing to follow. She regretted having wakened him; he had had a long day coordinating the resettlement of a fifty families into a newly-refurbished section of the catacombs that was near a tree garden, deep down, near the Pivot. The families would be tasked with tending the trees.

On the bridge, Bolos had Exocommunications on the main speaker.

"I'm here," said the voice she had heard so briefly, so many years ago, and never since. "I have arrived. Come to me. Come to me one and all, and let me drink in your glory."

Then, Sugra, manning Security, interrupted her. "Captain, I'm receiving word of an attack on Vadaris."

Vadaris was a magnificent new city, the first that had been built since the emigration of the Darkers. Much of it was still under construction, and much had already been built. It was being built properly, not haphazardly as Pelis and Bridgeton and most other cities that had been built in the bleak years after the Darker invasion had been. Vadaris was meant to be a testament to hope and to the future, a shining monument to what they could achieve. It was heavily populated, with a majority of the population being Flamers. Six hundred miles from Bridgeton, it backed up against the Chasm. The intent was to eventually construct a second Bridge across the gulf. But that was years in the future.

"Casualty reports trickling in," said Adler at Damage Control.

"So good, so...tasty," said the deep voice from Exocommunications.

Embra had a sinking feeling in the pit of her stomach. What if Jordan's Darker friend had been correct?

"Does God respond to you?" she asked Bolos.

"No."

For a long moment she stood indecisively, feeling as if the world were crumbling around her. Jolak could not have been telling the truth. God would not be against them! The mission could not come to this!

The voice of God, whispering blasphemies, suddenly shared the main speaker with a multitude of screams coming from Vadaris, piped into the speaker by Tava at Intraship Communications.

"Witnesses are describing something huge in the sky, attacking the city," Tava reported.

Just then, Jordan came onto the bridge. He took up an unobtrusive position as he always did, for he really had nothing to do on the bridge.

"I've got to go to Vadaris," Embra whispered to herself. Then, louder, so the others knew her intention, "I'm going to Vadaris. Maybe I can talk to God face to face, beg Him to stop."

"You still think it's God?" Jordan asked.

Without replying to him, she ordered Sugra, "Muster the troops and send them to Vadaris at once." The army was housed in the catacombs a hundred miles south of Bridgeton.

"Already en route," Sugra said, having anticipated Embra's order. "You'll get there first, though."

Embra nodded. To Telnon, she said, "Stop the Shaft when my ride docks, then send us on our way when I'm aboard. Stop us at Vadaris, of course."

"Yes, Captain."

She looked at Jordan. "Are you coming?"

"Of course," he said without hesitation.

They raced next door to Shaft Access.

After the Darkers had left and humanity was still re-discovering the world, they had discovered that the Shaft had a Counterbalance to keep the world stable and unaffected by the Shaft's rotation. Since the Shaft was just now approaching the opposite side of the world to Bridgeton, the

Counterbalance was approaching Bridgeton. It was simply a weighted "mini Shaft" that stuck up from the Pivot, its tip exactly even with the exterior hatch of the Shaft Access antechamber. On the flattened tip of the Counterbalance, the ancients had constructed a cabin with row upon row of seats, in which passengers could ride in comfort as they were whisked along to various locations around the planet. It was an efficient transportation system.

The Counterbalance arrived. Embra opened the exterior hatch, and she and Jordan boarded the cabin. Seconds later, the Shaft lurched into motion once again.

It was the longest trip Embra had yet taken on the Counterbalance. Of course, she had been all around the world on it, a trip which took twenty-four hours. Vadaris, though, was only six hundred miles away, taking just over an hour to reach. But for her, it was the longest trip because she fretted the entire time. God was attacking, and people were dying. She couldn't get there fast enough.

Why was God attacking? God was a benevolent being who had created them all. Such a being would never hurt them. Ergo, this being could not be God.

But how could it not be? The course etched into the Bridge Keeper's skull had led them here. How could the course have been etched into the skull if God had not willed it to be so? God had called to her ancestors on some faraway planet, and they had launched this worldship to answer that call and meet with God.

This moment was the culmination of that mission. They could not have come so far across the universe simply to be devoured by God.

Jolak could not have been right! Something was very wrong here.

She felt heat building within her.

Jordan took her hand, and they rode in silence. There had never been many words between them. They simply belonged together, and words weren't necessary to their relationship.

An hour later they arrived at Vadaris Station. Embra stepped over to an intercom on the cabin wall. "Telnon," she said. "Wait a couple of minutes, and then send the Counterbalance on its way. We can't let it be damaged in the attack."

He acknowledged her order.

She and Jordan disembarked onto the station, which was a long platform that clung to the sheer wall of the Chasm, thirty feet below the lip.

As they began climbing the ladder to the top of the Chasm wall, the Counterbalance glided smoothly away from the platform, quickly disappearing into the darkness.

When they came up over the lip of the Chasm, a scene of utter devastation greeted them. Vadaris was in ruins. The houses, the towers, the parks, the fountains — all had been practically razed to the ground, the metal plates ripped from the buildings and scattered to the winds, leaving girders cutting the night sky like jagged metal bones, and wood beams charred and smoking. There were fires all across the city where gas lines had exploded. Frightened people clambered deliriously among the ruins, coughing in the black smoke drifting on the gentle night breeze, seeking a place to hide, seeking escape, from the thing hovering in the sky.

It was lit from below by the thousands of fires scattered throughout the city, and from the light of Flamers that occasionally became tiny stars burning in the night. The thing was an enormous disembodied head, a ghastly visage, monstrously vast and hideous to behold, thousands upon thousands of feet high, thousands upon thousands wide. Far bigger than the city itself, too huge to take in with a single glance, and wildly distorted from Embra's perspective on the ground below it. She was like a mite standing beneath the head of a giant.

The head hovered a few hundred feet above the ground. Its face was made of a material that might have been white ceramic, painted with strange symbols in gaudy colors. Its eyes were black, its nose long and thin, its lips full and feminine.

The androgynous face was nestled at the center of a roiling nimbus blacker than the blackest night, shot through with orange flames and dancing sparks, almost as if the fabric of space itself were burning, breaking apart, and falling in toward the head. From that blackest of smoke, ten thousand tentacles issued forth, each at least a hundred feet in circumference, waving like stalks in an invisible breeze, undulating sinuously like the worms Embra used to hunt as a child in the water gardens of her Pen. The tips of the tentacles were belching smoke, feeding the nimbus surrounding the head.

The tentacles were grey, rubbery, segmented, and with enormously long reach. Even as she watched, wriggling clusters of them undulated toward the ground, seeking out the fleeing, screaming people. When any given tentacle neared someone, the person halted as if transfixed, and as the tip of the tentacle opened wide like some obscene mouth, the person burst into flame, engulfed in a ball of plasma fire upon which the mouth began to feed, sucking in the flames, drawing them off and up into the tendril, which seemed to function as a monstrous digestive tract.

All across the city, the tendrils fed upon the Flamers, while others prowled through the air and along the ground like hunting serpents. And all the while, the huge mouth smiled, the black eyes closed in ecstasy, the mouth moaned like a climaxing lover, the sound rolling thunderously across the landscape.

Those eyes opened when Embra climbed up from the Chasm. The head turned ponderously to face her as if blown by the wind. It began to drift toward her at a glacially slow rate. She could feel those eyes upon her even though they were totally black, lacking any pupils.

The ecstatic moans stopped, and the deep voice she had heard on the bridge reverberated across the landscape, thrumming in her very bones. "You have arrived, my nova," it said. "I have arrived. We have arrived together. Well met, fire of the heavens. Your people are morsels of light, and you, my prime morsel, my sweet. Feed me, slake my hunger for one precious moment, and power my flight toward the next star, which I shall savor in your honor."

Then it began to moan again, as it siphoned energy in through its thousand serpentine mouths. And a thousand of her people winked out across the blasted cityscape, even as a thousand more were found by the questing tendrils. And still the face loomed, drawing ever closer, inch by painfully slow inch, toward Embra.

She knew there was no reasoning with such hunger. The thing was hunger incarnate. Not God, she knew in her bones. Not God, her soul sighed ecstatically. This was a devil, a blight in God's universe. And she had been sent by God to smite it. She would expunge this black star from the heavens.

For she was the Flame Queen, God's Star (where had that thought come from?), and she felt something primal opening within herself. Instinct took over. All around her, in some dark mental space, stars flared to life. The stars that burned within her people. The Spark, the remnant of the stars from which they had come. She sensed them, a vast starscape within herself. All around the worldship, she called them to her, she triggered their flames. Everyone, Flame Kings, regular Flamers, even Ashenfolk, Jordan standing next to her — all burst into flame. And she drew in those flames. Four and a half million writhing tentacles of flame streaked toward her from everywhere around and in the world. The energy of a thousands suns converged upon her.

She merged the millions of flame streams together into one immense column of fire that she hurled at the ghastly face hovering in front of her. The starfire blasted a chunk from the face's cheek.

The ecstatic moan turned to a pained shriek, and the face reeled backward in shock.

Again she blasted it with a geyser of flame, and a crack appeared down the center of the vile face.

Again she blasted, and the lower left quarter of the face pulverized into a rain of fine powder that showered the ground beneath it.

The tendrils that were in the act of feeding upon her people convulsed, released their victims, who fell to the ground, burnt and withered husks. The face screamed in agony, and the tentacles retracted toward the black nimbus around the face.

Once more she lashed out, raking her inexhaustible fountain of flame across the face. Ceramic began to melt; the crack she had made became a gash.

The face began to withdraw, slowly rising away from the world. But too slowly, too late. She blasted it again, and the face broke in two. The halves fell away, slowly, so slowly toward the ground, as if gravity had only a tenuous hold upon them.

She blasted one half, and it exploded in a shower of debris.

Again she blasted, and the other half was likewise pulverized.

Now only the wriggling mass of tentacles remained, with an empty hollow place nestled among them where the gargantuan face had been embedded. And slowly, the tentacles shrank back into the roiling cloud of blackness until they were lost to sight and only the filthy black cloud remained.

She blasted the immense cloud, and it shivered. It pulsed and rippled as flame spread across it. It ignited, and burned until the flames consumed whatever foul substance composed it. Then the flames slowly died out, until the last of them rained to the ground as a shower of smoldering embers. In the end, nothing remained of the hideous thing that had dared call itself God.

Embra let her million-threaded blaze die out, and the flaming tendrils recoiled to their individual sources. All around the world, the stars she had called into life quiesced and became her people once more.

Beside her, Jordan's fire extinguished itself, and he dropped to the ground, naked, sweating, and gasping for breath.

Nearby, people were emerging from wherever they had taken shelter. They looked into the night sky with trepidation, fearful that the gargantuan murdering face would return.

But Embra knew it would not. She had slain it, just as she had been destined to do.

She took Jordan's hand and pointed at the nearby people. "Come on," she said. "Let's go help them."

# 24 - Looking to the Future

When the new day dawned, it was upon a world of smoke and ash. Vadaris had been laid waste. Surveying the damage, it occurred to Embra that there were some things the light could not make more beautiful after all. The people of Vadaris who had survived, most of them Ashenfolk, picked through the ruins in search of clothing to replace that which had been burned away during the first and last flaming they would likely ever experience. There was much weeping, and Embra left the city with a knot of grief in her heart.

It took her and Jordan a day and a half to return to Bridgeton. When she was at last back at her chair on the bridge, the final numbers were just coming in from Damage Control. Fifty-four thousand, five hundred and sixty-six lives had been lost in the night's disaster, most of them Flamers.

Embra declared a day of mourning and remembrance. Then the world began the dreadful task of laying the dead to rest. Not that there was much to lay to rest; the Devourer, as it was now being called, had drained practically every last atom of its victims from the universe, so there was nothing to place in the crypts.

Once the mournful days were over and the world was ready to move past the tragic event, and plans were underway to begin the rebuilding of Vadaris, Embra announced that the world must literally move on.

"Our voyage is not over," she said to her bridge crew. "We were launched with the intention of meeting God, and it is obvious that we have not. That unholy creature was not God, but merely an obstacle along our journey. In retrospect, I believe that God brought us here to slay the evil beast that was devouring His creation. We have done so. And now it is time to move on."

She held the old Bridge Keeper's skull aloft. "Three of the numbers on this skull provided our course to meet the Devourer. I believe the remaining three shall provide our course to meet God."

She stepped over to Astrogation and keyed in the last three numbers on the skull.

"Let's find out if I'm right," she said.

And she pressed 'Engage.'

9 798822 409271